DARKER THAN MY EYES

V. J. WAKS

CONTENTS

Hunger 1

Add on a Demon 31

Strange to Me Now 51

The Enemy Within 69

The Knife 131

© 2015 V. J. Waks. All rights reserved.
Bergerac/SapperTab Entertainment

Cover design by Scott Ross.

No part of this book may be reproduced, stored in retrieval system, or transmitted by any means without the written permission of the author.

ISBN: 978-1514399996

Because of the dynamic nature of the Internet, any Web addresses or links contained in this book may have changed since publication and may no longer be valid. The views expressed in this work are solely those of the author and do not necessarily reflect the views of the publisher, and the publisher hereby disclaims any responsibility for them.

There are sacraments of evil as well as good about us and we live and move ... in an unknown world, a place where there are caves and shadows and dwellers in twilight ...

ARTHUR MACHEN

HUNGER

We're scared now, Tom and me, so scared we don't dare leave each other alone, not even for a second.

Scared enough to have to keep the lights on all night, even in just our little set of rooms, as low as they are, flickering like they're ready to quit forever, risking bringing the whole system down. Both of us scared because we no longer wonder which one of us is going to go out to it, we know which of us will stand up, all simple, uncaring, completely calm and at ease – and walk out to it. To whatever it is that's out there, in the compound itself. In the dark. Whatever it is that's been slowly killing us.

That was four days ago, it started.

There were five of us then, all good men. Sound. Not a crazy one among us. Close, like guys get, working together, living almost in each other's shoes because in jungle this thick, you don't take chances. You lean on the guy next to you. He leans on you.

That's the way you stay alive. And it was working real fine; we were almost done with it, done with the heat and the sweat and that feeling of being all closed in, even when you stepped outside the tents. All closed in, especially then. All ready to pack up our gear and go home.

Four days ago. Out of nowhere. It was Nick, the tall guy, as good on a computer as he was on a baseball diamond. Team leader, triple degrees in AniSci, Plant Biotech and Evo. You couldn't touch him, he was as hard as a plank of white oak. He went first, four days ago.

It was midnight. We'd all just finished the last test run on the new water samples we'd pulled. Nick just stood up, calm as you please, like he was going to take a walk in the jungle, all wild, loud green, like every jungle is, even in the dark, like he was going out to take a leak. Easy and relaxed. He ran his big hands through that thick, blond hair of his and smiled, like he wasn't as tired as the rest of us, with the last week of round the clock tests.

"Well," he said. "That's enough for me. Time to eat."

He stood up, six some-odd feet of him, the ironman, and started for the door of our makeshift lab. Robbie, our Exobiologist from Houston, all bright, brown eyes, and twitchy limbs like a spider, he actually laughed at him.

"Where you going? You hungry again? ... we just ate, what ... like an hour ago."

Nick's cool Nordic gaze clouded over a moment and he stared at Robbie like he didn't know him, as though Robbie had called him back from a place where only he stood, way apart from the rest of us, miles away from where he stood now.

"What?" he said.

"Where you going, man?"

"Dinner," Nick answered, and his forehead was all puckered, his voice soft and strange. "It's time. Time to eat ..."

What a joke, we thought. And as we laughed at him, not really seeing it, not thinking, he walked out the door into the night. We should have known somehow, somehow we should have guessed, when we saw that look in those usually clear-blue-lake eyes, when a man we knew as solid, uncompromising genius suddenly started acting like half his mind was gone.

We never saw him again. Oh, we looked, not realising the danger we were in, even looking, if we had stumbled on it out there in the night. Next morning, we found his clothes. They were torn to pieces. Shredded and nearly pulverized into a damp powder, they were nothing but a slick paste of gummy fabric and something else; wetter than they should have been, even with last night's light rain.

But no Nick. We took his stuff in.

It was Stan who thought to run some biochem on them, Stan, our top Physio man, one of the best rugby players at Cornell, who later that night called us all together, standing there looking at him like a bunch of disbelieving owls, while he told us what he'd found or thought he'd found, impossible as it seemed. That the stuff on Nick's clothes wasn't water, wasn't sweat, not even blood, at least not blood from a man or any other animal or plant he knew before.

That was the night, the night that the sounds of the jungle around us stopped. That noise you'd get used to hearing all around you, night and day, all the time. It came to a still, breathless halt outside the compound itself, stopped dead, like you'd cut off the voice and heart of every damn living thing within ten clicks of here. Like suddenly nothing was out there now, nothing was in the jungle but us. Us and something else; that night, Stan walked out to meet it.

It was late again. We were all sitting together, moody, edgy, thinking about Nick, wondering, some of us, me even, plain worried. The silence was thick enough to taste. Like a warm, heavy blanket over us, dark and uncanny. That, and more; it was the feeling that there was something there.

Something in the dark; somewhere close by, maybe even in one of the buildings nearby, we only had three real buildings, none of them big. And the refuse and storage areas, they were always so cluttered and hard to sort through even when we knew what we were looking for, even when we weren't scared – anything could have been in there, waiting. Something that moved, if it moved at all, so quietly; like the dry creak of an otherwise well-oiled door, always moving just before you touched it, making a sound always just beyond the edge of hearing. It took Stan next.

He got up from the mess table and walked to the window, looking out at the supply crates and storage tanks, all tumbled together, not sixty feet away. The lights were working reliably then, but dim, like they always were at night to save power.

You couldn't see much out there that night, not even on those nights when the light from a full moon would somehow pierce the canopy and get down to us here in the valley.

But we could see he was looking at those crates like he could see something there among them, something darker than the shadows. Yet he didn't say a word, not even a frown on that rugged face; and next to me Tom laughed, a little weakly because he was drinking again, what with Nick gone and what the hell to do about that stuff on those clothes.

"Now don't you tell us you're going out to take a walk, too?"

Stan turned and stared at him, stared through him. He looked back at all of us like he was looking at video; eyes dull, glazed, calm as you want.

"Yeah; I think I will …"

What do I know? Me, I'm just the numbers guy, the resident Stat nerd. I don't know what I was thinking, what any of us were thinking.

But as I watched him I could feel the fear starting to rise in me like nausea, cold and unstoppable. Stan was a firecracker; I'd never seen him like this, almost dazed, his mind a mile away. Tom stood up and I jumped up.

"Don't go out there, Stan."

"Why not? It's time; time to eat. Hungry ... It's time."

And he walked right out the door.

For a second, Tom, Robbie and me, we were simply thunderstruck. We just stared at the door, then at each other. Then we ran after him. He was gone. Nowhere. We went out, staying together, our voices too loud in that terrible stillness, now afraid of the dark outside our dimly lit, silent little island. Afraid of what was out there – in here with us.

What could we have done? What could anyone have done, there was no way to understand it, to even guess what might happen next.

There was never any time – it never gave us time to think. Stuff was coming too fast.

Too fast. Now it was Robbie; he's the one who trashed the radio and comm system.

It was next day and totally without any warning at all. One minute he stood there at the table, his bright eyes gone all dim and flat, looking at the radio, just staring down at it like he'd asked it a question and was waiting for it to answer. Seconds later, with both Tom and me practically at his throat, he was still swearing he hadn't done it, even though we'd watched him, frozen in disbelief, as he'd pulled the unit to pieces almost in front of us. He swore he hadn't done it and his eyes were stony, unblinking, almost unseeing the whole time. Just like Nick's had been; just like Stan's.

So we locked him up. We didn't have to lay a hand on him. Quiet, unresponsive, walking like a clockwork creature, he followed us like a lamb into the ready room and that's where we left him, calm and still, locked behind closed doors.

While Tom and me, armed to the teeth, went through the whole place together, with a fine tooth comb, looking for god knows what.

We didn't find a thing. No, I mean it – we found nothing at all. No insects, no birds, not a single living thing. Nothing but hot, green, jungle, here where the animal species count was in the thousands, the most densely populated spot in the whole damn delta.

Again the eerie silence. But now – horrible, even thicker, like something alive, right in your face – silence now in the full light of day.

And we both felt it now, both of us without even having to say a word.

There was something there, something growing out there, all around us, growing like a plant with a rich, new, food source, growing as fast as any plant, as hungry as any animal. That's why the other creatures left, they knew something was there, too. They had the sense to leave.

It was already late day when we finally realised that we were losing the generators, they were going out on us and we were damned if we could figure out why. Tom worked for hours on the system and all we knew for sure was that we'd have lights that night but not really for sure and maybe not all where we needed them. And when we finished, tired, the fear starting to grow in us again, even as the daylight slipped away, we looked back into the conference room to check on Robbie.

There he stood, all pissed. He was laughing, as sane as either one of us, demanding to know what the hell had happened, why we'd locked him up in there alone. And when Tom told him, his face was utter astonishment, like we were telling him a story, describing crazy events and even crazier actions that had happened to someone else.

So we let him out, and started praying, not just for him, but for all of us, hoping we could get through another night all in one piece. So we could make a run for it. But by that time, it was already dark.

Like every time before, it was real late.

We were all in the mess tent again; staying close to one another, trying not to look at the windows, trying not to look at anything but each other, jittery. Listening for the next silent call. Because it seemed too unbelievable that it wouldn't come, that whatever was out there in the dark would let any of us get away.

"We have to get out of here. While we still can. I don't think we have a choice," I said. But Robbie looked at me kind of strangely. It was only a quick glance; then he looked away. Tom and I locked eyes and we waited.

"What ... what are you thinking, Robbie? Huh? tell me, man," said Tom, and his voice was casual, so smooth, not showing a shred of the fear I knew was growing in him, like it was growing in me, a cold, hard knot.

"Oh, I don't know. I just think ... I don't think we should leave. Why should we leave? "

And he looked at us with those brown eyes suddenly glazed, as cold and empty as a fish's.

This time it was much worse. Because both Tom and I were watching him, we were waiting for it, waiting for Robbie to straighten suddenly, slowly, almost imperceptibly stiffening in his chair. His head came up, and in a heartbeat, he was a stranger; rigid, straining in his seat.

He seemed to be listening for something only he could hear, while outside, the silence did something impossible, something silence couldn't do in any normal world, not in any sane universe, not in any universe we knew.

Because outside the tent, it actually seemed to get quieter; quieter and quieter until it was so still that the silence seemed like something alive, palpable, solid.

The silence spoke and Robbie was the only one who could understand the words in that horrible speech.

And with the lights beginning to flicker, so dim we could hardly see, both Tom and I were on our feet long before he started to rise, slowly and mechanically, to his. We grabbed him, yanking hard on the man who, eyes staring ahead, staring at nothing, was ready to move to the door, to walk through the door to where that unknown, impossible silence called, hungering for yet one more of us. And so strong was that call that even with the two of us hanging on him, terrified, desperately calling his name like two panicked kids, tearing at him as hard as we could, he pulled us along with him, dragged us to the very brink of the door that led beyond into some kind of voracious, incomprehensible hell. We fought him, fought with every ounce of our strength to hold him, and still he dragged us with him.

I don't know what god it was that stopped him, there before the door. It sure as hell wasn't us. It was with empty, sightless eyes that he was now staring through the window, exactly like the others had stared before him. He turned to us, all gentle, mild as milk, and he spoke to us and his voice was as low and as hollow as a corpse's.

"I'll be going now. It's time to eat. Have to … *come out. Come … come out …*"

And in a sudden icy fear, I looked out the window, following the line of those cold, unblinking eyes – to the storage areas just across the way, into the doorway which led beyond to the little tarp-covered holding area.

I looked out to see something there that shouldn't have been there, that wasn't there, not in any normal sense of the word. And I was so frozen with fear, me, a fucking man of science, rock stable in any world of wonder, I was so afraid that when I finally spoke, I could barely get out a whisper. But Tom heard me.

"The door ... look at the door. Tom ... do you see it, Tom?"

It took an eternity of two seconds before he could get out his answer, and his voice was hoarse and horrible and I knew he felt what I did at the sight, at the impossible sight of that unhallowed thing in the shadows under the tarp.

"Yeah. Yeah, I see it ..."

Robbie stood there at the door, Tom and me beside him, with our fists white-knuckled and knotted in his clothes, and we all looked out to the doorway under the tarp, with the lights flickering on and off, as the generator caught and choked, to where something darker than the shadows stood. Rounded, low to the ground, like a figure but not a figure of anything I knew, short, dense, unmoving. And even though none of us could see them, there were eyes in that dark mass, watching us, aware, still. Hungry. And all of us knew that whatever we were looking at was not a man, not a figure of anything we knew at all, and whatever it was, it was still growing, growing as fast as a plant, as hungry as any animal.

"Don't you see it, Robbie? You can't go out there ... *my god, Robbie!*"

And in some kind of desperate fury, I lost it. I hit him; hit him hard, hard enough to hurt him. I know I hurt him. I heard him gasp, once, hard, his breath like a shot in tent.

The lights in the compound actually flashed; flashed and stayed on; once, real fast, like a really bad stage joke. Incredibly, Robbie roused a moment. For just one split second I thought we had him back, I thought we had him.

Then he was gone. He looked at us again, placid, once more calm, unruffled and without blinking an eye, he grabbed the gun from my belt, raised it and pointed it straight at us as we drew back, away from him; drew back in horror from the man who would have killed us if we tried to save him from the thing standing out there, waiting for him, darker than the shadows. We kept backing until there was some twenty feet of room between us when the lights failed utterly and in the total terrifying darkness, I heard the gun hit the floor and the sound of the door opening and closing. And I flew to it, to that sound of the door closing, stumbling blindly forward into the hard chairs, shoving them out of my way, fighting to get to the door, to get out there into the dark after him.

Tom caught me just as I reached the door. By now, the entire compound was out, totally in darkness now. No moon that night; no stars through the thick canopy. So black was it that there was no sign of the tarp or the thing under it and I fought him, struggling against Tom's grip that was keeping me inside, his voice loud, like thunder in my ears next to that horrible, knowing silence.

"No! You can't save him, not that way! It's too late! He's gone!"

"Let me go! Let go of me, you son of a bitch!"

And I hit at him, fought him as hard as I could, trying to get out that door as, without warning, the lights came on again, came on full and bright, blinding us both. My last sight was of Tom's fist coming straight at me, right into my face and I dropped, senseless, not even feeling it when I hit the floor.

It was just beginning to get light when I came to.

I was propped up against the wall of the mess tent, neck cramped, with my head splitting.

I could hear Tom beside me. He was talking in a low whisper, his voice so soft, so strange, that it took me a few moments of hard listening before I could make out what he was saying. At first, I thought he was talking to me. Then I thought it was himself. I was wrong.

"Where are you going? Where do you go ... where do you wait — before you come to get us? It's getting light now. It's getting too light for you, isn't it?

You can't take it yet. Not yet. But soon ... maybe after you've had another one of us. Come back! You can hear me; I know you can! Come back, you son of a bitch, I'm gonna get you. I know how, now I know how to get you! I'm the one who's gonna get you for good."

Then he stopped talking because he could see I was watching him.

"You can hear it now, can't you," I said. "Like the others did. In your mind. It's there in your mind now, too, isn't it ..."

A full minute went by while he stared back at me without saying a word and the look on his face never changed. I looked into his red, tired eyes, looked at his drawn, white face. He looked like hell. I knew only then that he hadn't closed an eye all night. Then he glanced down and I saw that he still had the gun in his hand. When he finally spoke, he was still staring at that gun, staring at it as though it were a crucifix, never taking his eyes off it.

"I'm next."

He wouldn't tell me how he knew, how alone out of all of us, he was the only one who could hear it before the call actually came. Before it got dark. I don't think now that he actually knew the answers himself or even how he seemed to know with such absolute certainty what he needed to do now.

But he did know and as the day went by, the more I watched him, the more scared I got.

I could feel it, as plain as you can feel the winter's cold, the teeth of an icy, hungry wind all around you, picking away at your clothes, trying to get inside.

Something terrible was going to happen. It would happen very soon and it would be something much more horrible than our losing all these men, one after the other, losing them in silence and some kind of dreadful, killing calm. And this thing was something that Tom intended to do himself.

Because that was what it was – the calm, at least that was a big part of it, from the pieces I got from him, the hints that he let himself tell me, stuff that made me sick to hear it.

"It needs us to be calm; it can't take it when we 'feel' anything. Not yet anyway. And the dark – it still needs that, too. It makes the dark. The lights – you remember the way they dim, when it's out there, waiting? And how bright they got when you hit him, when you fought with Robbie ... just before ... It needs us to be still. No anger, no fear, to be almost dead inside ...otherwise ..."

He wouldn't say any more.

I tried, pushing him as far as I dared; all day long, my mind frantic to think of what I could possibly do, to help him, to stop him, to save him. What could I possibly do now at all? At the end, all I could do was follow him around and watch him while he walked back and forth across the compound; he was pacing the distance between the mess door and some spot just before the storage areas. And I saw he never passed a certain point – he always stopped before that doorway, where we'd seen it – and he wouldn't let me near the place at all. He stood there, just before the door, and he put out his hand as if he could feel something in the fabric of the air itself.

Then his hand would freeze like that; all his fingers out-stretched, still, reaching, until his hand finally dropped to his side. And it trembled.

But he wouldn't tell me. It was as though telling me might somehow expose me, let that thing get closer to me before he could be ready. Because the door in his head swung both ways, I saw that even then. And I saw it was taking everything he had to just get himself ready, to protect me and still not let that thing know what he had in his mind, what he was now ready to do. As it started to finally, inevitably– get dark.

Because it did start to get dark. That hungry, knowing darkness crept up and over us like it had before, but now it was just Tom and me left. And finally here we were together, both scared, all the lights on, knowing that we could only keep them on so long, that they wouldn't stay that way, that eventually that thing out there was going to suck the light out of our pitiful little rooms like it had ripped the life out of three good, strong, men.

My nerves were so hair-trigger raw by then that you'd think I'd have been ready for anything. And I thought I was ready; at the first sign, I was ready to move, I wasn't going to wait.

But neither was that thing out there. Before we could even light the hurricanes, vainly trying to stave off that darkness, to outsmart it – Tom cried out.

He dropped his lamp, and his hand went to his forehead, like he was in pain. And the lights, they were dimming even as he screamed, his eyes staring out, one second glazed and the next lucid, as he fought that thing that was calling to him. I ran to him; all I could think was to keep him inside but he threw me off, struggling with me as I fought to hold him, as he started laughing and the lights began to flash on again. In another second, he'd shoved me backward and I saw the knife in his hand, the one he always wore, his big Bowie, and its blade glittered in the dim glow of the one lamp we'd managed to light.

He glared at me, and frozen with horror I watched as he pulled the blade of that knife across his own arm, the bare skin opening, the blood rising bright and red even while the lights began to flash horribly, angrily, even stronger than before.

And the echo of that stillness outside – famished and reaching – it suddenly rose to a roar of silence, and I could hear the loud pop of sparks discharging out under the tarp, like some kind of mad lightning had suddenly touched down.

Tom's eyes glazed over again; he was fighting with every bit of his strength and as the blood ran down his arm, he gave a shout of triumph. He was moving to the door as I grabbed him again and when he tossed me backward this time, it left me crumpled up against the wall. He'd thrown me off him with the strength of many men, like with that one act he was saving my life and his own soul.

Even with the blood running into my eyes, I could see the lights dim as he tore through the door.

He was running as hard as he could out into the night and I could hear his feet pounding. He was shouting as he ran and they were shouts of rage and a wild mad joy and a lust to kill that thing that was waiting for him. I stumbled to my feet just as he reached the far side of the compound and once more, that horrible silence was coming alive.

But this time was different. This time, that thick, cloaking stillness had started to vibrate and hum. With no sound at all, the heavy dark air was throbbing with it, the air that was pulling itself out of my chest while the very thoughts in my head were humming with awful jarring pulses, one after the other.

The space in the doorway under the tarp crackled and roared like some kind of fabric was ripping apart and tearing itself open.

I heard him scream. That's how I knew he'd done it. None of the others, not Nick or Stan or even Robbie – none of them had been able to scream.

It was a scream of not just fear or pain but of real triumph that I heard and that's how I knew. And I was ready to run to him, to run out there into the dark, but I couldn't. I just stood there, just outside the door, holding onto it, trying to stay upright, trying to keep from screaming myself.

Because of what I heard after that long, last terrible cry from Tom. Because from out of the dark where I was going to run, even as Tom's voice died away, there came another roar. It was like a wind that grew and grew until all the air was throbbing with it, a sound of hate and despair, and a terrible hunger, like a great starving mouth had opened into hell and all these voices came out, all starving, all screaming at once.

And I stood there, shaking and crying because my ears hurt so bad, my skin was on fire, because it seemed that something unstoppable, a thing made of blackness and some terrible cold fire was eating into my mind. I stood there in agony, hardly able to stand, and suddenly – it was gone. Like a dark, cold, tearing wind that just hits you and then passes you by, and you look out, still standing, at a world gone mad, now quiet, now still. Like a door had opened and let damnation look out, then just as suddenly closed.

The lights were on again, blazing brightly all over the place when I finally stumbled forward, crawling almost on hands and knees until I found Tom.

He'd made it as far as the doorway under the tarp. That was where I found him, lying on the ground, face up, his sightless eyes staring up at the trees over us.

He'd gutted himself. He was sprawled just before the door, his white hands still on the hilt of the hunting knife sticking up out of his split rib cage and his flesh and abdomen gaped open almost to his groin, still bleeding, still warm.

Somehow, he'd had the strength to open himself up, to take that thing with him as he died. There were burn marks all over him, like he'd stood in flames or some kind of terrible heat and his body had been burned, almost charred by it. He'd been right; there was a smile on his face to light up even the deepest corner of any real hell, however dark.

There, not five feet away from him – what was left of it. A pile of something blacker than any midnight sky, black but bleeding redly, bleeding blood that was not its own. And I stood there crying like a child, and I watched it collapse inward, folding into itself, the blackness and blood shot with light that had no colour at all, wasn't light from any place I'd ever seen or dreamed. I watched as that blackness flickered and moved with light from some nightmare place where real light and human feeling was the enemy.

I breathed twice. And whatever was left of the thing under the tarp was gone.

And the whole jungle was getting light now and then I heard something that finally brought me to my knees, sobbing, not able to breathe with the sobs that came out of me.

It was the song of a bird.

A bird was singing high up in the canopy. It sang until the sun rose full up; it sang as if its heart was breaking with joy and pain, just like mine was. And its voice rose and soared, until all I could hear was that pure, clear voice and the voice of thousands of other living things once again – and the whole jungle was once more filled to overflowing with clean, wholesome, earthly light.

ADD ON A DEMON

I've always been this way.

Always; ever since I could remember. What was fun for me was trouble for everyone else, and I mean real trouble. I mean the kind that hurts people, not just in their heads. Mom and Dad put up with it all my life, most of theirs, too. It was never easy, never fun to watch 'cause this kind of life eats away at your mind, as well as your body.

Angry – all the time, that's what I was, with the kind of white hot anger that makes it easy for you to do the dumb thing, the thing that hurts. I can't remember not having it. It was with me all the time, since I was little, like a hot, sweet cloud over me. Me and that anger; what a pair we made – I was never alone. I wanted it that way; I needed it.

When I ended up in the corner for it, when I ended up in the principal's office or the police chief's – I was never alone.

Time at home was getting worse and worse, especially the last months. My folks left off even the odd two words. At just about the time my brushes with the law were getting serious, I guess they'd had it. As Mom and Dad were making decisions, I stayed under my cloud, like a thunderbolt just looking for the moment to strike. It was about the same time my girlfriend Amy was trying more than ever to help me. Prettiest girl I'd ever seen, with soft, smooth skin and a gorgeous long white throat. I don't know whose idea it was, maybe it was hers. We were the same age, just 17; she always cared about me. But, I'd been as much trouble for her as I'd been for my parents.

I don't blame her if it was her idea. Possession Therapy had been only the newest, hottest thing for kids like me for about five years now. It seems everyone knew someone who'd had it done.

That's a lot – most of the cases you heard about involved a kid, a troublemaker like me. And with about seventy five percent of the time, with the thing working – having the demon actually take hold – results were pretty good, I guess. Unless you were the kid who got one put in – a demon, I mean. Adding on a demon meant your good seed would get all roused up – what little good seed you had – and they say that all of us have some. Adding on a demon made that good seed try to protect itself and somehow get even better and stronger and take control.

You see, it was all relative – if you were bad and got something worse put into you, somehow you got better, and it was reliable, predictable in that percentage. That's how they figured it, that's why they figured it worked so well, so often. That little voice, the one that had always been there in your head, telling you to go ahead, do the fun thing, the dumb thing, no matter how stupid, how bad it might be for the rest of the world – that voice somehow got scared and ran.

When they put the demon in you, that voice finally shut up. That's why it worked so well, so often. A new voice would start up as you fought with the thing, that new voice told you to be stronger, be smarter now, more responsible and moral and all that crap. I mean, the worst that could happen was that the damn thing wouldn't take, and you'd be left just where you were, where you started.

At least, that's what they figured.

What none of them fully realized, not even Amy, was how happy I was just where I was. I didn't want to be helped. Life was already good, perfect even. I had that white-hot anger – I didn't really need anything else. Not even Amy really, even when she was turning herself inside out trying to fix me, to get me to change. She never understood just how much I didn't want to be fixed. Not one of them saw this, not my folks, not the State Therapist who'd been chatting with me for years, who had finally approved the procedure, not even the State Deacon who supervised the demon transfer itself.

It happened on one sweet, gloriously sunny day in the spring. The folks had got me to come downstairs with some cock and bull story that we were all going out for a hot dog. That was a lie, of course; I knew it was a lie. I knew; I may have been bad but I've never been stupid. I knew something was up right when I got to the hall at the bottom of those stairs, way before the Deacon's guys all marched in. I blackened both my Dad's eyes before they stunned me. Next thing I knew I was sitting on the floor, blinking, and babbling, and cursing while they put the cuffs on me. The lies kept coming: how it was the only way, how I'd feel so much better – that I'd be so much better afterward. I heard Mom crying in the background; couldn't tell if it was for me or for Dad, or for herself.

I can't tell you how it was even done. They don't let you wake up, not fully, before it starts. What I can say, is that when I came to, half in and half out of hardly awake, I knew I was lying down, flat on my back. I could feel that for sure.

But I couldn't move. No part of me, not my arms or legs or my head. I couldn't open my eyes. But I was aware, you know, the way you are when you're half asleep, out lying in the hammock on one of those perfect summer afternoons. For a second, I was warm, all loose and easy; I even thought I could hear the bees in the garden, and the birds up in the trees, chattering around me. Then I suddenly knew I wasn't anywhere near a garden, not mine or anyone else's.

'Cause it got cold.

It got so cold around me that the air hurt to breathe it in.

Everything went still. There was silence; that came first.

It wasn't like any silence I had ever known before. It was silence with colour in it; a terrible stillness, like there was something way back, deep inside the silence, where the blackest part of it would be. There was something back there. It was alive and it was thinking and waiting, so at home in the dark, so empty, so cold with awful hunger.

What came next was a whisper of a sound – it was a human voice. It was the Deacon's voice, whispering, calling, he was whispering in words that weren't English. Hell, they weren't even Latin but something so old, so much older – a filthy language from long, long ago, filthy and horrible. His voice got lower yet louder, the words echoing like his voice was miles away. Yet somehow I could see them, the words he was whispering. I could see them as well as I see you, there they were— etched in the dark. His words were just like flame. They burned like the dark, like some ice-cold flame. The words burned me, and I could see them in my mind, like they were alive.

It got colder then, if that was possible; it was now like I was caught, tied and helpless in a silent, unmoving blast of air that was nearly solid with cold.

And back there, in the darkness where all the emptiness and hunger of this whole damn sorry world was concentrated – something was waiting. Something was stirring and coming alive. Back there, something slowly began to move.

Then it woke up completely – I could hear it moving, the rustling of its skin was like the brittle rustling of dried leaves, like leather that was ready to crumble, a thousand, thousand years old. The thing moved, blacker than the blackness around it and damn, I could see it moving, raising what could only be a head.

Then it looked straight at me. The Deacon's voice was gone. Yet his words were still there, frozen, hanging in the darkness like icy spears, like lightning bolts of frozen live flame – and now I was alone, there in the dark. Alone – except for the Thing that had awakened. That *he* had awakened.

The demon rose up – it rose up and started to climb, up out of the darkness. I could hear it clear, the sound as it rose up, standing now darker than the dark – and its eyes opened wide and I could see them, like fire in ice, so cold, so frozen. And I couldn't move, I couldn't scream, I couldn't get away, and its footsteps echoed like soft, rolling thunder that got closer and closer. It was right over me then, and the eyes, my God, its eyes were like nothing I can say, I will go to my grave seeing those eyes. I was choking, choking with cold that seared and burned and I couldn't breathe with the cold and the weight of the thing as it lowered over me. Its claws reached out, reached out of the darkness – for me – and as I fought to breathe, to scream, its hand covered my mouth, that hand, so cold, so hard, so inescapable, its claws reached out and covered me with the stench of the open tomb.

I woke up – if you can call it that, at home, in my own bed, in my own room.

Everything was exactly where I'd left it. My desk was still a mess – someone had tidied it but it takes years to mess up a desk like that, it'd take centuries to clear it up completely. Life doesn't work that way, does it? Like a sorry little giggle, the light still trickled in at the windows as it always did, pushing its way through those dumb lace curtains my Mom had put up one horrible birthday, when I could call myself a real teen, about a thousand years ago.

Groggy and sore, I peeped over at those windows now and I suddenly remembered – how there had been a sparrow that would always come to the windowsill. He'd been around all summer, almost every day. Amazing; when he saw me come to the window, up he'd fly. Then he would pop in and wait on the sill; I always had bread for him. I trained him; I'm good at training things. I had been feeding him that very day, the day they came to the house. I was thinking how much I wanted to see my sparrow – how much I wanted him. Right now, though, there wasn't a bird or anything else on the sill. Strange, that somehow I could hear that bird, even if I couldn't see him.

Not so strange maybe that I felt different.

Everything got different that day, one way or another. It was different now – I could hear a bird that wasn't there and right across the room from me, right in my own room – there was the State Therapist, the one who had given the okay on my case. He was sitting in a chair by my desk. He'd been reading something, a Bible I guess, judging by the roughed up cover caused by years of frantic, scared shitless thumbing. He was still reading when I finally opened my eyes, wider but careful-like, and I looked him over, all fifty odd years of him with a suit that barely covered his paunch. I smiled. I was wondering; if he dropped the good book on the floor, would it open to all the juicy parts, like some good stroke book would?

He seemed to feel my eyes on him. He actually stiffened in the oddest, most satisfying way in his chair, like a dirty little shadow had fallen across his nice clean white page. Then he looked up, straight at me, and slowly closed his book. I felt a little pang of something

– call if mercy if you like –and I softened my eyes a bit. It must have helped.

"My dearest son," he said. "We give thanks that you have been returned to us. It is a new day for you. Your life is just now beginning."

A new day, a new life; indeed, it was. I smiled again. It was a good smile, I was feeling pretty good. Yet it still seemed to shake him a little. He looked closer at me; he frowned, tried to speak. Then he cleared his throat instead, as the door flew open. My folks must have been right outside – in a heartbeat, the room was full of people, all crowding around me. I was sitting up now, on the edge of the bed. I was quiet, they had been told to expect that, that would have told them a lot. There I was, smiling and relaxed; that, too, was a sign. I was surprised myself, I just felt so good, better than I had in years. And I kept feeling good, even better and better, for the next two days, while I got more and more polite and helpful and just plain nice.

Everybody noticed it. Everybody beamed, they were all so happy, so relieved, when I told them the truth, that for once in my life I felt like a whole person. It was absolutely the truth.

It wasn't all of it.

As lost as I had been before, stumbling around in my head and my heart – the truth is that, now, suddenly – I was just so much more on track; cool, calm and collected.

That is what I told them.

What I didn't tell them about was the anger.

That's what I didn't tell them about. How that anger, the feeling that had been white-hot and sweet, which I'd felt and had been close to, every day of my life – had somehow changed. Of course it had, hadn't it? Wouldn't you have thought it? I mean, everybody did. I was so different, so much better. Surely, something had gone. I mean, it was obvious.

Of course, it was.

But the anger hadn't gone.

It had just ... changed.

It wasn't white-hot anymore – now it was cool, cold, getting colder, it seemed, every day.

And what I also didn't tell them was how there was something new in my mind. How, every night now, as I drifted off to sleep, there was something new, something different. There in my mind, every night, they were there, getting brighter and brighter with each sunset, with each coming of the dark.

The eyes.

They were the same eyes I'd seen shining out of the dark, when I had been lying there, helpless, tied to that bed. The same eyes – and night after night, they got closer and closer. Redder, they got, and friendlier, too, like that anger that had turned cold, and friendlier and calming, somehow. Once again, more than ever, I was never alone. I was still covered by a cloud, a cloud that kept me focused and ready to work, there's so much work to be done. I was ready now to work, to take care of loose ends, you know? We all have them; now I saw mine so clear, with a cold pleasure the likes of which I'd never felt before. Every night I was never alone, and every morning, I just got happier and happier, with a sense of deep, abiding peace and a calm I'd never felt before in this life, or in any other.

But I missed my sparrow. I wanted him and one day when I was in my room, damn if he didn't come back. There he was, there on the sill, ready for food, and I went to him. Afterward, hours later, after I'd left and when I came back from my walk, I went up the stairs to that room and wouldn't you know it – there was Mom.

She'd found them, of course, the feathers – in the bathroom. There was only one really, one that I'd missed. The sparrow was long gone, nothing to see of him at all – except for a small spot of blood. That was on my shirt collar, I'd missed that, too. But no matter; I had that shirt collar turned under before she could even notice it.

I told her all about it, how I'd found him on the floor, that somehow the bird must have hit the window. But everything was all right now – I'd taken good care of him. You should have seen it – I held open my arms, and she came straight to me, right into my arms. I held her close. She went all relaxed, there in my arms. She was so grateful, so happy I was there, I thought for a minute she was going to cry, just like she'd cried on the day they took me.

I thought of that day as I held her.

I could see the two of us, there in the mirror.

I was smiling; I was watching us in the mirror, together, so close. There she was in my arms. But she couldn't see me. So she never saw my face – my smiling face with those eyes, those eyes with that soft light shining out of them, like a sweet, rosy glow.

The very next day, who should show up but the State Deacon himself; seems like he and the State Therapist had had a little chat. The Therapist himself showed up right on his heels, and now they both went in to sit with my folks. I puttered around the closed door until they all came out and the two guys left. Something about the final report; we never did see it but my Dad looked at me, hard. He looked at me hard, straight into my eyes, watching me, studying me, thinking hard – and I knew. He didn't say a word; it was Mom who told me how the State folks had suddenly had some doubts about what they had done to me, how maybe it hadn't actually taken at all. That was crazy, wasn't it? I never felt better in my life. I was fine. Even my folks thought so; at least my Mom did. That report was coming, it would be ready real soon; the Deacon himself was going to come back with it in a few more days – and they would talk more.

In the meantime, there was work to do, lots of work – I missed Amy. I really wanted to see her again.

I did, too, that very night. I showed her a good time. She deserved it, she'd been the one who had stuck by me so long; such a special lady. Amy always loved me before and she really loved me now.

So we went out, we went dancing, at a place we'd never been to before. Then, we went back to her place, 'cause her folks were out. After some really nice love-making, tender and sweet, she was all soft and relaxed in my arms. I kissed her. I kissed her lips and I kissed her throat, that soft, white throat I adored. And with just my hands, with no effort at all, I snapped that throat like it was a twig. She never felt a thing. I made sure of that, and I made sure she was taken care of as well. There's a real pretty spot off the cliffs near our house. That's where she went over. It's gorgeous down there, down in that valley – it was the perfect spot for a girl like that, as special as Amy.

Life was still good, getting better and better, at least for me. But life is funny, you know, what's good for some folks isn't at all good for others, it seems.

Dad had an accident, just a few days ago. It was pretty sudden, totally unexpected. He was at the bottom of the stairs when Mom found him – right at the same place they had finally put the cuffs on me, that glorious day when they wrestled me down, to take me away. His neck was broken, he must have died at once – I knew he hadn't suffered, that's what I told them. It seemed to help; even the Deacon looked like he felt better – oh, yes, he did come back, with the report, and he and Mom talked for a good, long time.

Mom is still crying a lot; she misses Dad. It's just the two of us now. I hold her close. She calms down a lot, there in my arms. I hold her until she calms, until she is still and calm, as calm as I am. It seems to help. She tells me it would make her happy if I went back, had the whole thing done over, that's what the Deacon advised. He's a good man – so useful.

I don't mind going back in again – going back down again.

That's what the Deacon says I should do; he's sure it will be different this time, so much easier.

I know he's right because that's what the Demon says, too; that this will be even better for me, for Us. I know He's right – there's plenty of room for more, so many more – in me – in Us.

We're going back down tomorrow; I can hardly wait.

There's so much more work for me to do, for Us to do. At some point, I'll try and find some time to take care of the Deacon. Yet I know there are other kids, kids just like me. They need my help – they need Our help – they should go down, too. That comes first.

But for now, I hold my Mom close; Mom with her throat so white, so soft. I'm ready; I'm getting more ready. My life is just beginning.

Humans are so trusting, so fragile.

I give thanks for that; We give thanks.

We give thanks for that – to all the Gods – save One.

STRANGE TO ME NOW

I can't tell you when I first began to notice it.

In a small town like this, change is such a quiet thing. A slow thing, it creeps forward like some blind beast. Feeling its way forward, it lumbers on, padding silently, stealthily. Until one day, you wake up and something has changed.

It might have started the night with all the lights. In the sky; meteorites, they said. It was like heaven itself was falling. Falling like so many white-hot little coins, the stars fell. In streams, across the whole damn jet black sky, they went right over where you stood. It was mid-summer, the kind of southern night that was warm and humid. The air was heavy with that sweet smell of moist, new-cut grass and jasmine. Lots of folks were out of doors that night. It's the way we do in small towns, setting outdoors, enjoying our porches and the song of the crickets and the simple smug pleasure of having no more than a hundred people nearby, and knowing all of them fairly well.

I was out that night, too; me, and Cutty, my dog. Fine dog, a purebred mongrel, and as sweet a friend as anyone could want, especially if you were getting on in years and in fact wouldn't see sixty again.

I found him in the road after one particularly busy Memorial Day; I guess someone had had too much barbecue, and had been none too careful with their car. He was busted up pretty bad, but I'd got him to the vet and he'd mended just fine.

Better than I had, what with the bullet I took in the war and the scars and now the losing fight with arthritis and what. I lost a lot of myself with that bullet, that and the way I was treated, and still am, like someone who just doesn't count anymore. It never changes – it's always about their lies; they need to have a scapegoat for everything – that was what I saw, then and now. To hear them tell it, everything was wrong with me.

I'm not done hating them for that; I still have loads of hate left. My friend Al tells me it's going to get me some day. He's a widower; no family, keeps mostly to himself, he has no one to lose. I stay close to Al because he needs it. I was close to him that night, the one with all the lights.

We were sitting on his porch, Al and me and the dog, sipping iced tea and just talking. Tim stopped by for a bit. He had a bite and a sip, then he was off like a shot, the way kids do. He was an orphan, staying with an aunt who had too much time for herself, and almost none left over to take notice of a young boy coming and going from her house. That night, with crumbs on his face and his eyes bright, Tim took off down the road. We could still hear him laughing, his young voice high and floating in the dark, and Al and I were just getting into why some folks do what they do, when we saw them – those falling stars.

"Well, will you look at that," he'd said. Al had leaned forward, staring from his rocker. Then he stood up and walked right out to the edge of the porch. I got myself up, too, my hips and knees aching from sitting too long in the damp night. There we stood together, looking up at the sky.

At the lights.

Like you could touch them, those pinpoints of light flickered down in an iridescent show above the house. I don't think the whole thing lasted more than a full minute. One minute, there they were, up there like some kind of flag or some big, glowing announcement. You had a chance to feel wonder, and the next second they were gone. It was something.

We sat down and chatted a bit more and I made my way back home. Whether it was from the lights or the talk, I just couldn't sleep that night. Oh, I tried all right. Tossing and turning and putting my fist into my pillows, with the dog's warm weight across my legs at the foot of the bed and him looking at me like he wished I'd drop off soon. For hours I fidgeted. I looked at the clock again – no help there, it was around two. It seemed I finally got the right spot; it was when I settled down that the first stuff started.

Quiet the house was, the way houses get quiet deep into a summer night. Even the crickets had had enough and gone still. But something woke me; I blinked and looked round and then I saw him.

Cutty had sat up in the bed. Now he stared at the door that led into the hall. His head swiveled about until he was staring at the wall, the one just opposite the bed and I knew that he was listening, too.

That was when I heard it. Just a soft little creak, like the wood in the wall itself had shifted or settled. It was only the smallest of sounds and it lasted no more than a split-second. Then Cutty turned twice, and I thought we were both settling down. It was right about then; that was when we heard the something else.

It was coming through the ceiling right over the bed, down from the roof itself, and try as I might, I know I won't be able to say how it was. It was like just before you fall asleep, when you're right at the edge of a dream. You hear it, the noise something small makes if it were soft and flabby, and didn't move real well, or maybe it couldn't hold on to an old, pitched, shingle roof that might be slick with dew. That was what I heard, the sound of something moving across the roof; soft, quiet, not like a rat or squirrel or raccoon or anything I'd ever heard before. Whatever it was, it wasn't running or anything like that – it moved like it didn't care if I heard it or not.

Cutty heard it too; he slowly stood up on the bed, looking like he was trying to stare a hole through the ceiling.

He didn't make a sound.

But, even in the dark I could see the fur lifted all down the length of his back, even in the dark I could see him trembling.

The noises stopped and the rest of the night sounds came back, one by one. Cutty sat down again and when he asked to go out I let him; I left him on the porch. I was suddenly sleepy and the clock was heading on toward four. I guess I never even made it back into the bed. Somehow, I remembered to close the front door and before I knew it, I was out on the living room sofa, out cold.

I slept like a log, better than I had in a while. I got up at first light with the birds singing, a little stiff from the couch. Couldn't see the dog anywhere, then I recalled – damn, did I really leave him out all night? I was calling for him as I went to the door and opened it. I went out onto my porch and there I found Cutty.

He was dead. Curled up nose to tail, he was cold and stiff, like he'd lain down to take a nap sometime before dawn and just hadn't woken up. When I got down to him, there on the deck I could see something was wrong. His snout was all strange, the soft leather of his nose, usually so moist and smooth was wrinkled up and shrunken. The loose skin of his jowls, all that skin was tight and dry now. Tight and puckered it was. Pinched, almost like tanned leather. All the rest of his skin, all over his body, it was like that too; puckered and stiff, dry but with a cold, clammy feel.

His eyes were still open.

But they were filmed over. What had once been soft wet, friendly brown was now grey and leathery. It was as if he'd put his face right into the hot steam from a pan of boiling water and his eyes had been all scalded away.

I felt real bad, like something terrible had got hold of me, just short of my knowing what it was. My stomach was all sick but I couldn't leave him there, was too sore to heave him up. I found a length of old rope, tied it round his neck and dragged him off the porch. He went into the ground behind the house, in the garden, good and deep. I stood there a bit and I sighed over the mound of dirt that finally covered him.

I went back inside and as I passed the hall mirror, I stopped in my tracks and stared.

Stared at myself.

Where once had been hair thinning and grey, I now saw new growth, not a lot but as dark and rich a brown as I'd seen there when I was twenty. There were still lines on my face and the skin was still loose, falling into the folds you'd see in a man of my sixty some-odd years. But the colour of the skin was fresh, and when I lifted my hands, hardly able to feel my own face for the shaking, I could feel the skin was soft and almost smooth. The ache in my wrists, that same ache I'd been feeling almost constant now for years, that seemed suddenly different – like the edge was taken off.

I didn't know what to think. It was as if time had turned backward for me, while it had surged forward for Cutty. A man my age imagines a lot of stuff, stuff he dreams of having and being. Then again, maybe he doesn't.

But I needed to keep busy. After two long, hot, hopeless days trying to work around a dog-shaped hole in my life, and what- the- hell about those changes in me, I finished up my chores for the day and then I heard Al calling to me from my porch.

He came in; he was real sorry about Cutty. He looked at me hard, said I seemed different somehow – that was all. I'd fix us both some supper. We stayed up late after dinner, talking for hours, mostly about everything and nothing. He said Tim had asked after me, what with the boy not seeing me around and all. Tim was a fine kid; Al wished he was his. It seemed a good thing for Al to stay over so he bunked on my couch. I settled him in with a blanket and got myself cleaned up. The house got all quiet; we turned in and I fell asleep listening to the crickets.

Next thing I knew it was well after midnight; it was the quiet that had once more woke me up.

I lay in bed – listening. It got quiet outside, like before.

I half sat up – there they were again, the sounds on the roof, like before, and once more they were coming through the ceiling over the bedroom. But they seemed different this time. Now the tread of whatever was up there was clearer, stronger, like whatever it was knew where it was going. The sounds crossed the roof slow but steady toward my side of the house; then they stopped.

Hoping for a breeze, I had left the window open.

Now, in the dark, I could see the glimmer of the light from outside, the moon was near past full. Now, in the dark, there was a darker shape there at the window, silhouetted, right on the sill. I'd never heard it get there, but there it was. It was small; I couldn't make out what it was. When it hunched itself up then moved, like it was feeling its way over the sill, for a second, just a second – I thought my heart would stop.

That lasted only a second – in the next breath, I'd calmed down. I was still calm when it left the sill, when I could see a small, dark shape slowly making its way up the wall, and along the ceiling. I was falling asleep as it left my room, moving across the wall to vanish near the ceiling of the hallway.

That night I slept better than I had in years. Nest day my head was clear, even my morning stretch seemed good and easy. I don't remember actually going into the living room to see if Al was up yet. All I remember was suddenly finding myself on my knees on the carpet there, looking at him lying on the couch. He was dead; cold and stiff, just like Cutty had been. Just like Cutty, his face was dried, puckered, almost caved in and all his skin on his body was shriveled and tight.

I just stared at him for a bit.

I was all mixed up between god- awful fear and sorrow.

Somehow, I got myself up; I turned away from the sofa and banged straight into the wall near the door, trying to walk and still keep sight of what was on the couch. That mirror that had hung there for twenty years came down, right off the wall, only the carpet and me saving it from breaking. I slid down onto the floor, my back against the wall. I sat there, I picked up the mirror, the thing shaking in my hands – and I stared again – at myself.

It was even worse than before – because it was so much better.

I couldn't remember the last time I looked this way, with my face all young and smooth, my hair so thick and full, my eyes so bright.

It took everything I had to put that mirror back on the wall.

But I was strong now. I got another length of rope. I had no trouble at all getting Al off the couch and out the door, into the back; no trouble at all digging the spot for him. Al had had no one, he would barely be missed; he was my friend and I took care of him.

That night, when the quiet came again, and then the sounds, stronger and louder than ever before, and this time – not one but two shapes, both dark and silent were on the windowsill again – I could barely remember ever being scared, not ever before. And when I felt the bed move, shifting, when I felt that soft pressure, that warm weight across my legs at the foot of the bed – all of it seemed right. I was sleeping soundly, long before the night sounds started back up again.

I was so fit the next day, even in the heat, I was out chopping wood, cleaning up the place like a man half my age. I was so busy that the day sped away and it was nearly twilight when I heard the call from my porch – there was little Tim, all smiles and jokes and eager talk. He wanted to be sure I was okay; I asked him in for a snack and we caught up. He looked at me as if he was trying to place something in my face, maybe something that seemed to him different, but he never said a word about it. Before we knew it, it was dark and suppertime, and no, his aunt would hardly mind if he stayed to supper – she would hardly notice at all. I remember having some wine; I don't recall how the boy got into it. All I do know is that he was at the table one moment and dozing on the couch the next, and I went in to rest on my bed; wine does make me sleepy. I hardly turned my side, even after the bed shifted again, long after midnight.

Next morning, it was hard to see him like that, Tim.

There on the couch, he was the same as Al and the dog had been. I couldn't leave him like that, alone, with no one hardly remembering to worry if he didn't come home at night. I carried him outside to the back, him like a dried husk, as light as a feather in my arms. He, and Al, and Cutty keep company. All I knew was that I was strong and young now, better than ever before, younger than ever before. I no longer wonder at it; I keep my windows open at night.

I got busy again, happy with the way time passed and with what I could do. It took nearly two weeks before they came to my door, the men. They had questions. I went with them; I had nothing to hide. They took me at my word; I guess they brought Al, Cutty, and Tim away from the house.

So here I am in this room, just over in town. I stay here, and I wait, and I marvel at it – at how far I've come.

Strange to me now, the days I lived before, the nights of pain, the life alone.

Strange to me now, the way I had been; it was fading from my mind, like the memories of clouds that pass; all I can see is how I am now.

They tell me the ropes they took off the dog, off Al – that they were put on before they all died. Well, that's just nonsense. They tell me I don't look any different than I ever did before; that's a crock, too. How would they know? I feel worlds different – if I'm not different, why do they look at me like that? It never changes; it's always the same, same as before. This is nothing more than lies, their need for a scapegoat.

What's different is that what they say doesn't bother me anymore.

What's changed is me.

They say I'll be in here for a spell.

Not for much longer, I know.

I have new friends now, good and strong. They won't want me to stay away too long. I can't help thinking that they know I'm here – last night, even in here – I heard the sounds on the roof again. There may be bars, but I can still keep my windows open at night.

I'll get out. Then I'll go home, or maybe to a different one – stronger than I ever was before. There are not a whole lot of things wrong with me anymore.

There may not be too many dogs left in the place; I guess folks have a need to put their money elsewhere.

But there are still plenty of children.

And we can always make more.

THE ENEMY WITHIN

"And why are you here?"

"My aunt knows the judge. It was either this or incarceration."

The Chief stared at me like he'd either swallowed the wrong end of a fork or he'd heard it once too many times before.

I looked back – as best I could. I'd nearly lost an eye, you see. Well, it's there but it doesn't work worth shit. You don't need to know how. It shouldn't have happened; the usual bad to worse progression, from suicidal ideations to acting out. One day, all the wrongness finally crystallised solid inside me – and I hauled a driver out of his vehicle and went after him with a crowbar.

Funny thing, anger; what it does to you, where it takes you.

It's a trip down a rabbit hole that starts with a clear-eyed, clear-minded young adult wondering where the system went wrong.

It becomes the pit that leaves you unable to choke down any more of it, the unfairness of it all. You're down there alone, unable to cope with being left out, left behind, just this side of crippled. It ends with the rest of the world looking at you then looking away with a pity that kills – so it can go merrily on.

Why didn't I just cope? Well, let's see; which one of the twenty odd legitimate reasons would you like? Ask me that again when you stand there.

I'll just say, we never really know what the words mean until we get there, until it's too late.

I finally snapped that last thread of despair on a sunny day on the cliffs, having fled the scene of a near slaughter. I'm not a killer; somehow that day, I stood in a new pair of shoes, a strange pair, where murder seemed okay. I could justify it; I could live with it even – it didn't touch me at all.

So I ran; to the cliffs. I looked past Dover and out to that blur on the horizon, the Channel telemetry towers that line the ports at Calais, there to keep the migrants from crossing. Blue sky, clouds like castles, the sea like glass. I didn't see any of it; not those chalk white cliffs, not the damn gulls. All I saw was most of it going away, my life going away.

So there I stood on grass as short as my options; I stood there with a good friend, a loaded 9mm – I was still a crack shot with almost any weapon, even with the left eye almost gone – and I wondered how I got to – *here* – ready to use that friend on myself.

I didn't, of course. They came and got me off the cliff and I went to trial.

I was saved by the slimmest of margins, if you can call it being saved. The guy I almost killed was a pedophile wanted Federation wide. He went to a hospital and then to a cell; he wouldn't be saying too much about me. The Court would see to that; it was my aunt, you see. Bless her heart; she always had a soft spot for me. Me, the odd bird, the girl who wouldn't play girl's games, the one who re-wrote the boy's games, always too smart for her mouth, always one step behind real genius, one step ahead of a holding cell.

Fame comes in strange ways.

It turned out I did have some genius left, just not what my aunt, or I, or society would invite over for a family dinner.

There were places that could have some use for me – for that anger I still had. The charges would drop, the case would disappear – if I recruited.

So I sat and smiled at the half hour of counseling, at the Court ordered physical and hair cut. I was going to do community service of a very special kind, a service on a grand, dark, bloody scale, where my street smarts, where my aptitude with a side arm would be appreciated – where my anger would be useful to all. I smiled and I packed – and I shipped out to OW626, the training way-station between here and the Belts.

I had nowhere else I wanted to go. Out of sight was what they wanted; out of mind was what I got.

"Belligerent; that's what you are."

I stared at him and tried to keep confrontation out of my eyes. It's what I felt, of course.

Decatur was the kind of man, the kind of Chief that inspired that kind of knee jerk reaction, at least in someone like me. In other recruits, I could see how blind obedience and blind fear could be other alternatives; never blind loyalty. He was clearly on his way to something else, something bigger, maybe an LB, a real Base. For now, he was here, large as life and twice as natural. He was all ours.

He wouldn't see thirty again. Yet, not a paunch in sight; it was hard muscle all over him, top to toe. Decatur would have been eye candy even in civvies; the uniform of a Spec Chief, a Special Warfare Command

Instructor just underlined the obvious: the maleness, that in- your- face certainty of him knowing who he was. He liked the guy inside there, in that uniform.

I knew for sure I wasn't going to.

Something about his eyes; the look as that gaze passed over me. Like I was just so much territory he was assigned to, the next field assignment he had to move over. Somehow, like the belligerence he saw in me wasn't a virtue, not an asset but an impediment somehow.

I wasn't here to learn fucking etiquette. I was here to learn how to kill – better. How could it not be an asset?

I blinked twice, just like any female would do, to put a little sex card right before us. He rose to it; his eyes narrowed – and his desk comm sounded. His eyes stayed on me as he spoke into it.

"Yeah, Gillie. Ok; come."

A guy came into the office; he'd be Admin. Tall, lean, like everyone here, like rations were part and parcel of the gig. Gillie's eyes went over me anyway; the Chief went aside to talk with him. They stood there, looking over a digifile; chatted, while I took in more of the scenery, the space of my commanding officer.

To my right and left, the walls were as blank as the Chief's expression, the space as empty of warmth as the eyes that had passed over me. There were no images, not a single file tab open on the wide desk. He'd had to rise from that desk to meet Gillie. When they turned away from me, I could see the rest of the counter behind his chair. It was plain – except for the object that would have been right behind him as he worked.

I was getting real glad the two of them hadn't an eye on me just then.

I swallowed my amazement, my disgust – my fascination – and finally tore my eyes from it. Oblivious to my regard, exquisitely mounted, perfectly preserved and set on its stand of dark apparently real wood – was a head.

If it had been anywhere but here, I'd have said it was a replica. Knowing the man who had it, even as little as I did then, this wouldn't be likely.

The skin was smooth, stretched over a skull that had to be intact. The eyes, large and wide set, were closed as though in sleep. I had no idea then what colour the irises would have been when alive. I couldn't have told you what I know now – about the pupils that would have been only slightly different than mine – the texture of the face so akin to mine that not one in a hundred from my home planet, my home town could have pointed out a difference. A soft smile was laid in there in the dead flesh.

Hideous, fascinating – riveting – this possession, like the man already capable of instilling fear, exacting attention – this head put to rest most of the doubt I had had about what drove this man, what he considered important.

I had never seen an alien before; I would only imagine what the rest of the body might look like – how this trophy had been taken.

I wouldn't have long to wait.

Gillie saluted and left; Decatur turned back to me.

I didn't drop my eyes or my stance. He came right up to me. His eyes narrowed; he got conversational and I could smell the scent of him – he'd worked out, hard – some time earlier. Spec Chief Decatur's voice started friendly. It stiffened up right after, just like his jaw and maybe like the rest of him did.

"I know why you're here; how you got here. But do you know why I opted to let you stay?"

"No, sir."

"No, sir – Spec Chief."

"No, sir, Spec Chief … sir."

There went the jaw again. If it locked any tighter he was going to split a molar and maybe spit it right at me.

"We get 'volunteers' all the time. That's what our criminal justice system is for. That said, we don't get 'volunteers' like *you* every day. The kind we get fall into a few well defined types, classes, if you will. Stop me when any of this sounds familiar."

"Yes, sir, Spec Chief.

"The first kind thinks they're winners; that somehow they just got in the wrong game. They think they can still beat the system, the training, the instructors. You getting a warm, fuzzy from this group?"

I didn't answer; he nodded.

"Didn't think so. The second group, well, that one's a little different. More complex. *Different*. They may or may not be winners; if they are, it's because the game is in their *head* – they're writing their own rules. How about that group, recruit?"

My eyes had narrowed; he nodded again – but there was a new look in those cold grey eyes.

"Yeah; you're not in the first group. I'm kind of glad – kind of sorry – because if you were– I was going to grind you into pulp."

He was close enough to touch me now. The eyes had a much better view of the territory.

His hand rose up toward me.

I don't remember taking his wrist, my fingers gripping as hard as I could.

I don't even recall reaching for him – one second his hand was coming toward my face, the next I had him by the wrist, my fingers clamped over his heart and lung points – and my other hand, palm up, was under his chin – ready to snap his head back. He couldn't move, he was standing like a statue; across that eye - candy face was now disbelief, shock, anger – and pain. I didn't move either; we stared at one another for a cold, hard count to three.

I let him go and stepped back, both my hands clasped loosely behind my back, at attention.

He shook off what must have been real serious numbness in the hand I had let go. He chewed a fine looking lip.

"We're going to do just fine," he said. "Dismissed."

As crisp and as blank as fresh linen – I saluted and left the room.

I walked out the door, and straight into Tango.

I didn't know her name at the time; all I know is I'd been full of that anger and had slammed into her hard enough to put her flat on her back on the floor, all tossed limbs and fury.

"What the hell is your problem? What, are you blind? You can't be – or you wouldn't be here."

In point of fact, I hadn't seen her; she'd come up on that blind side. A little something snapped inside me – I get that a lot – still. I looked down on her and all I saw was red. I hauled her up by her ensign's shirt and dragged her right up to my face.

"As a matter of actual fact – I *can't* see. But guess what – *I'm still here*. So you can be damn sure I'm still good enough at something."

She stared at me hard; I stared back and under that look I let her go. She dusted herself off; her eyes never left me.

"Well, all right then; you've made your case. I'm sorry. I just had my ass kicked in the CTF."

It must have shown on my face.

"You must be squeaky new; that's short for Combat Training Facility, where we …"

"Train," I said. "I just had a close call myself."

We were still outside the Chief's door; her eyes went from me to that door and back.

"Oh yeah? Who won?"

The pout of my lips said it all; Tango grinned.

"A draw is good – here, a draw means you get to wake up the next day and do it all over again. Well, now. You can call me Tango. Let's go find us a drink."

Over that drink I heard a story I was to hear a lot; just how many of us were here because we had nowhere else to go.

The theme would be the same – it was this place or a place much worse – and the skill sets always matched the mission.

The mission was death.

The details came the next morning at Intake Plus.

Once again, I had the pleasure of seeing Chief Decatur in action. He was in his element, with two dozen odd recruits in a captive audience. Tango – her last name was Ariel, but she danced so well in a fight she ended up with a fine moniker – saw what I saw; we'd been assigned seats, arranged in groups – tight little teams. Standing by the walls were the Officers, their steely-eyed demeanor went clear to the bone.

Decatur strolled past us in a pin-drop still room. He was the parade; in front of us was everything he wanted us to be – everything we never could be. It was lose/lose across the board. Nothing existed other than his voice. I looked across the room to the Officers then looked twice.

My eyes had stayed on the tall guy there, the one who seemed the spitting image of the CO.

"Brother?" I offered.

Tango smiled. "He sure as Hell isn't sister."

"Damn straight."

"We call him Diamond; when Decatur steps back, he's the one who steps forward."

While I wondered, Decatur had gone down two lists; he talked while I made it real clear I didn't give a damn that his eyes went to me and Tango, over and over, as if he liked the idea of these two dice together.

"Four squads – six men apiece. You'll find your Instructor's name at the top of your sheets. You all here (and he waved at me and Tango and four other lucky souls) – you're with me. You will be tested, continually, in everything. If you pass, along the way we will evaluate you for our own particular specs and sub specs: sniper, close quarter, breach, demo, covert and tech. We start now; we're going to learn how to kill."

From somewhere in the rear, the question floated up.

"Who are we going to practice on?"

You can't imagine the look in his eyes as they went across the room, at the faces there in the seats. Those eyes came back and stopped on me. He smiled; it wasn't pretty.

"I can't wait to show you."

It wouldn't happen overnight.

Nothing does – not healing, not scars. Six weeks of merciless physical training went fast – there had been times I wasn't sure if I just wanted to die, my body hurt so bad. It had been pretty much what you're seeing in your head right now – climbing, swimming, physical combat with hell knows how many Instructors. And always we came back to Squad Leader – the Chief, and usually Diamond was right there with him. Decatur never changed; his eyes were as glacial, as covert as ice while he worked us bloody. He watched, measured, evaluated and judged – he had each of us in his toils.

Were we getting tough or just numb? Not a week had passed since the Chief had raked Cosmo over the coals for catching two breaths after a 5k run with gear. Cosmo's thing was playing with explosives. He'd practiced on a family's home, then shipped out here. I wasn't sure if the guy was going to cry or kill Decatur where he stood. He did neither. Crush, he was hard-core – he'd come from what used to be Hong Kong – he never even blinked an eye when Decatur socked Cosmo smack in the diaphragm. Cos is big, they still grow them that way in the North – his face went red then white. He sank down onto his knees. Count of three he came back up, stiffer than steel.

We all came up onto our feet; we had to.

By all I mean my squad, not the others. I was younger than most; me and Tango did ok. The others not so good. We lost three from the other squads the first week; one girl coded – bad heart. More dropped out from injury; some from psychosis. At the end of six weeks, the attrition rate was stable, at thirty percent. We did okay; the guts and glory took us to round two.

"Here– is where it all happens."

Decatur had brought us all in before lunch. He knew; no one could do this on a full stomach.

It was an arena, ten meters below the guardrail where we stood. It widened into an oblong, twenty meters wide, nearly fifty long. Weapons were scattered along the sides; some on the walls, many on the floor. Between the dried brown smears, I saw an intercom box there on the wall. Tango's eyes went over the space – over this Pit – I heard her whisper.

"Look at the blood."

Visible even from up here – spots darkened the edge of blade, cudgel, and staff.

Diamond was standing downrail from the Chief. We had two other Officers on the rails as well; they ignored the CO's brother the way guys do when they really don't like the other fellow but they respect him – or it's their ass.

Polidor muttered, a little too loud for safety.

"So how do we get down there?"

Decatur looked at him; a quick smile came to his face. Then he grabbed Poli midsection, hauled him over to the rail – and flung him ass over teakettle into the Pit. The guy didn't even have time to curse. We all rushed to the rail. There he was – clinging to an iron hand grip set into the side of the wall, a handhold.

I didn't wait.

I vaulted the rail and went over. There were handholds hammered into the walls, all along the place, up and down from rails to floor. I grabbed the nearest, grappled and rappelled with my hands until I reached Poli – then used him to steady myself until I dropped to the floor. He was okay; I grabbed the nearest staff, solid wood – the blade heads had been removed – and minded my own head, Decatur was literally flinging recruits over the rails. One girl broke her ankle on impact; she would be out for who knew how long.

But there were still some of us standing when the lights started flashing and the doors at the far end of the Pit growled – and opened.

Five Offs hurtled out of the tunnel beyond that door. I knew the name, not the reality – the Offs – these were aliens, the 'offscours' of society, maybe theirs, ours for sure. They were from planets out on the edge of the Rim, displaced by our wars, our need for more and more space, for more and more of everything.

These were probably from OEIII – the most like our world in the Rim's Belt and loaded with primates. The Offs had been on the losing end of the last two decades of conflicts – no one called them wars anymore.

In a conflict you didn't have to observe any Convention Agreements. Not that we would anyway; as victors, we'd been calling most of the shots for years, certainly for my lifetime. These Offs were humanoid – so like us they'd have been hard to distinguish from the real deal in combat.

"When I call time – everyone stops where they are, and I mean everyone," shouted the Chief.

"Great," spat Poli; he was still pissed about the wall plunge. "We stop – but will they?"

Decatur's eyes were on the aliens.

"These are the enemy. If you don't kill them – they will kill you. They fight by the same rules we do. Have fun."

Along with Diamond and the Officers, the Chief stayed at the rail; we didn't need to see him to know he was there, watching. So this was how it was to be; this is how we would learn to kill – how we would learn to stay alive. The Offs knew the game; they would most assuredly fight by the rules because it meant a ticket out – out of bondage, out of what must have been holding cells at the end of that dark tunnel – it meant another chance at life, at freedom – maybe even a chance to go home.

I didn't wait. As the Offs separated, making a scramble for weapons, I was already racing forward. The enemy charged us; my staff caught the first under his chin; it didn't kill him but he went down. I planted the end of the staff, vaulted around it and kicked – that sent the next Off to the floor.

I scooped up a knife; it went into my belt at the back. I kept the staff; distance keeping was going to be prime here. I shouted for Tango; over the din she heard and turned and came to me in a flash. We paired up and I looked up; there was Decatur at the rail. He had his arms crossed loose across his chest; Diamond stood next to him. They shared a word; both sets of cold eyes were on me and Tango.

I had about a second to meet the next Off head on. He was tall, taller than the rest and he had a staff, too – expertly he smashed aside my thrusts, one after the next.

"Nice one," he muttered.

"Fuck you," I growled.

"Anytime, soldier." And I flung the point of my weapon straight at his face – he just barely parried.

"You ready to die?" I asked.

He actually laughed; his hair, longer than mine and dark, fell across his forehead.

"You ready to get smart? *Where's last year's recruits?*"

I stared for a full second.

"What?"

It hadn't been his question that made my jaw drop, that had put a hole in my attention – it was the dizzying realization that I'd never seen a recruit from a prior year – only us, and our trainers.

It had never occurred to me to ask.

The Off didn't waste it. He vaulted over the edge of his staff and kicked me in the chest. I went down; he came down to chat.

"So – where are they?"

Without thinking, I punched him hard in the face; he went over, ass over tea kettle again – I planted my staff in the hollow of his bare throat as Decatur bellowed from the rails.

"Time! All weapons down!"

Offs were dropping their weapons where they stood; then they moved away from us, as the lights went to normal, as our Officers came down from the rails.

I got a look at my alien. He laughed, real low and deep, from the floor – it was a bitter sound, with a bitter grin. The lips, and the face I had seen before – they were the same lips and face as on the dead head in Chief's office.

Those eyes glowed up at me from the floor – and now I knew what an alien's eyes looked like.

"Who the fuck are you?" I whispered.

"You can call me Djan."

I wasn't thinking – I held out my hand – he took it and I yanked him up. Djan stood on his feet, right in front of me, and a hard look passed between us. Those alien eyes flicked to the side – to Decatur watching at the rail.

Slow, with every bit of insult he could cram into those sauntering, measured steps, Djan turned and stalked away from me, back to the tunnel, back to the cells, with the others.

I had never fought an alien before.

Everything about them was the same as us — only the slightest differences around the eyes, in the pupils, the hands maybe. I hadn't had the luxury to study this specimen, this alien – this man.

But his word – his taunt – it all stayed with me. Could it be that they shipped everyone out the second they could? Could it be they started fresh each time? It didn't make sense; no one could learn that fast. As careful as I could, I looked. As quiet as I could, I asked. They were nowhere. There was no one from last year's crop of misfits, not anywhere on the Base.

I couldn't tell you how my days had passed since I had met a most remarkable creature in the Pit.

But Djan stayed in my mind; I wasn't going native, not by a long shot. But the look in his eyes, golden eyes, the sound of his voice, so low and deep – and what he'd said – what that all led to, directly or indirectly, hung on to me like a bad cold.

They'd switched us out on the schedules; I was out of the Pit and on the range, training with Diamond. Tango had Decatur all to herself. She and I met at mess and compared notes; from what she could see, he wasn't quite as glacial as I'd thought. Somehow, this little remark, coming over a table at mess, didn't make me sleep any easier.

I'd already seen how too much power, in the hands of too few could screw things up. In a gang, it was a sure set up for a kill. Here the outcome might be just as deadly. Tango and me, we were still the girls in this year's crop. That automatically changed the dice, if not the game.

My days on the range with the Chief's brother kept me focused. I had to be; I made sure I was busy. My world was nothing but aim, reload, fire from the floor, lose and recover the weapon. I used that mantra to keep myself apart, from him – I stayed apart, as me – I lost track of the exploits of the rest of my squad.

It was on the range, last day, when Diamond's eyes were a little too bright, a little too in my face, like he was hoping real bad I would answer a question he hadn't asked.

My weapon jammed. We were firing ultra loads; the pistol was heavy, designed to spit out an insane number of rounds in the blink of an eye. A jam was catastrophic; if the shooter wasn't spot on, it might explode the round cartridge right in your fucking hand.

So, jam – my first one – Diamond was right there.

"Hold."

His voice was low, urgent; he was right next to me. I stopped where I stood. His hands went over mine – finger by finger, he lifted each of mine – then real gentle, real careful, he lifted the gun out of my hands.

His hands were sweating; mine, no less – I could smell the sweat coming off of him as he cleared the jam, pivoted the chamber housing, worked the safety – and dropped the jammed round and cartridge into his other hand. We both finally took a breath; he was pissed with the gun.

"Fucking things are too dicey; time and again, we've told them. They're accidents waiting to happen."

"So – why do we use them?"

He stared at me; he stayed where he was, right off my port quarter. His eyes went over my face, just like the Chief's had, like his brother's had at intake. He was measuring me, just like Decatur had, right there, and damn, I still couldn't be sure if it was for a coffin or a mattress. He took another hard breath; this one was different than that last one.

"Because we're told to. We do what we're told here."

I wasn't sure where this was going. Somehow we seemed to have jumped the track that the weapon issue was on, so I just threw it out.

"So – if someone tells you to use one of them on yourself – you do it?"

That stopped him. It wasn't just desire in there now, it was anger. No one talked to this guy this way. His voice went low and meaningful – with the emphasis on mean.

"If you want to get out of here alive – you do what you're told."

I let a moment's silence do its dirty work.

"Thanks for your help – sir."

The mood shifted.

"My pleasure – and it's Diamond."

It was night and a few days later, that Tango got up off my floor.

She'd stretched long and hard and still felt sick to her stomach. Training did that to you and we'd been training extra hard, primarily hand to hand, since that first episode in the Pit.

Cosmo was behind her; he was still sweaty, stretched across the sofa in my room. Vache snored from his spot by the table.

I actually had a sofa. Somehow I'd gotten sweet quarters. Not only wasn't I bunking with the rest of the squad, I had nearly twice the space. That had to be the CO's work; it didn't exactly make me feel all warm and cozy.

Special you are – but in a bad way. Stay frosty.

"Espy," came the voice from the floor.

I hunkered down and stretched out beside Tango; she really wasn't ready to try her legs.

It had taken the squad a full minute to get used to my name. Once they knew of course, it was easy – Espy – short for an even shorter acronym – s. p. – 'sucker punch'. It would be something I got to be infamous for long before I'd ever come to Base.

"We've done a bit of snooping, Vache and me," Tango murmured. She didn't have to be cold with anyone; Vache was the third of our legs in our little unit within the unit. Fast as hell – good looking too, despite or maybe because of the scars. He was scarred everywhere, a real street fighter, a mole inside a street cartel who got a little too close to the real part of the deal. So he ended up here; Poli was on the floor dozing too, just past the edge of the sofa. Crush was somewhere dallying; he would stop by later.

I looked them over. Tango, Cosmo, Vache, Polidor – somehow we all came together – it had all come together. I was never the kind to make friends with people I saw every day. I had never gotten close just because someone stood behind me in line.

I had never been part of a team. Cooperation, trust, watching someone's back … these were mystery, a magic I'd never known before. Here we were, all training together, as indies; as a team. We were the only ones we could trust to try to kill us, who would still stop before anyone actually died.

"What did you find, Tango?"

"I didn't. It was Vache. There are files in the Chief's office."

I shook my head. "They must be in the floor boards; I never saw a thing at Intake."

She moved, cursed with the effort, and turned onto her side to face me.

"They're there; and Vache knows how to get to them."

Finally, the rest of the guys scraped themselves off my floor and left. Tango and I talked more; I had always wondered about the road that had taken her here. I never asked; I also never imagined she would share what she did.

She had another sip of her drink; her eyes got softer.

"It was Donny – my sister. Donaghue Ariel; she was Donny to me from the time I could talk. I always wanted to be like her."

"Why?" I asked.

"Because she is a winner. Donny was always the winner; I was always the loser. The one who threw my life away, the stupid one, who screwed up, who couldn't follow orders to save my skin – couldn't stay out of prison.

"How'd you get here, Tango?"

"I killed two guys. You don't need to know how – it was just wrong. I went to prison; Donny went to training for real – real military, legit."

"Where is she now?"

"She's at one of the big LB's training to be a real soldier."

I looked at her; she wasn't shedding a tear. This was a story from long ago, one she was as used to as the colour of her eyes.

"You are a real soldier, Tango."

This time there was a little catch in her voice, like a new part had been added to the story.

"No; I'm not. None of us are – well, maybe you are – maybe someday. If I'm smart, I'll get through this place and get to an LB, a real Base, where I can be real – real like her."

I shook my head. I tossed out her drink; poured clear water into her glass.

"Does she know how much you love her?"

That actually stopped the tears filling her eyes.

"Don't know, Espy. She didn't leave me – I left her."

Since that day in the Pit, since the day Djan had thrown that question into my face like a fist, it had been the same savage little circle.

The closer we got to data, the tighter and harder that circle turned. We had started the area of inquiry with the Officers, mostly as jokes. We got nowhere; the next level would be the Chief; there would be no way that would play. We needed to know for sure, somehow.

There was a helluva lot of stuff going through my head by the time I got back to the next session in the Pit. I'd learned a few tricks in the month that had flown by. I knew what I wanted. I wanted info. I also wanted someone to fight with.

I wanted Djan.

I could only hope he hadn't been tossed to the sharks in some other unit's training session. The possibility he might have been hurt or killed bothered me somehow. He had fought me hard, fought for his life, just like I had. We were well matched as foes, maybe as ... It was what might come after those three little dots that stopped me. I was sure no one who'd trained here was thinking what I was thinking. I can't tell you what was going through my mind when I got to the Pit floor and saw Djan barreling straight at me from the entry doors. I sidestepped his charge, grabbed him and slammed him onto the deck, then let him pull me down.

"How do you know about the recruits?" I growled as I punched him in the face. His fist came at me. I dodged and he tossed me across the floor. I wrapped both legs around him as he came up with a knife – and raked it across my arm. A quick punch saved my shoulder; he was close enough for me to topple him onto his face.

"Because I've fought with them – for three seasons."

"And you're still alive?"

His legs came across and toppled me down.

"You call this a life?"

"It will be in one season more," I said.

"Won't happen. They'll never let me get out of here alive."

The point of my blade dragged across his belly – dark blood marked his shirt as my knife stopped a centimeter from his throat.

"Time!"

The Chief was silent at the guardrail; once more Diamond was at his side.

Again, my gaze locked with the alien's. Again, Djan's gaze went to the Chief – and back to me. There was no doubt; Decatur was feared and despised here; he was for sure on the kill list for every one of the Off worlds. The Off hauled himself upright; the point of his knife went into the floor between us. His other hand slowly released its hold on my shirt.

Both of us were breathing hard; both bloodied. The golden eyes so close to mine shone with malice. There was nothing but threat in his voice.

"Next time."

I looked into those eyes; I couldn't look away.

"Stay alive," I said. It surprised us both.

His eyes widened; the gold positively changed colour as he looked at me, looked into me. Then Djan looked up. Those up at the rails were his enemies. The Chief watched him as Djan spat on the floor at my feet. My own hand moved, rising in an obscene gesture – to the Off.

Djan left with the rest of the Offs. I left with my team.

Our next intel session was the eye-opener.

We already knew who we were going against in the Pit – the Offs. What we hadn't learned was how; how the undesirables of the System who'd had the misfortune to lose would come every year to Base – as our training tools. If they made it four seasons running, they had a ticket out of the Base for good. They might even find a place in our own ranks.

I laughed at this last bit; it seemed just like the best story to tell, the promise of freedom via combat. The Offs were still scum; it would be a death match every time we went in.

No one said anything about how many style points an Off would get if he killed a recruit.

The Offs and what we did with them were only part of the picture.

It really was hell out there; the Belts in the Rim were already deadly, thick with pirates and mercenaries who'd happily plunder any planet, any place not strong enough to fight, not smart enough to parley. They were a ragged set of crews, with fighters from all the worlds. They knew their business; pirates had been hitting the planets with the highest tech profiles for the last half decade. It was anyone's guess what poor bastards would get reamed next.

So much for intel.

It started to go south for me right about then – with a feeling in my gut that a shoe was somehow going to drop. That shoe dropped next day, whatever you want to call that artificial day/night that a rotating battle station inflicted on your body and psyche.

I'd come from somewhere, headed somewhere else; when you live on a Base like this, even if it's outside Regulation, it's corridors and more corridors. Eventually you find the sweet spots.

It might have been the lounge, where even recruits could chill and indulge in a little sip of short-term amnesia. I'd come out alone; down the opposite way, I heard a voice, two then, and then a bit of soft protest. I looked down – there, half-hidden in an alcove – was Tango. She wasn't solo. It was dark in there; the guy who stepped just into the light was Decatur.

I'd learned pretty damn fast; this was training. You do what you can with whomever they want. Easy; nothing serious here at all. That went both ways – except for Officers. In the light of that alcove, the Chief looked a lot more like a man than he had in his office. I went on my way – then caught up with Tango at mess again.

Good thing it was late but still loud and noisy; my little world changed for me that night.

She was alone at a table; I sat. Chat went on until I couldn't take it anymore.

"Listen," I said. "We all do whatever we can get away with. But if you're planning what I think you are – don't. It's not that he's too old, or too rough. It's his rank that makes this no good."

Tango didn't look up. Her face went white, like I'd slapped her.

"Are you jealous?" she said finally.

"Are you crazy? I can still see, with only one eye. You're blind with two; you can have any guy on Base. You don't need the likes of Decatur."

"I know what I'm doing, Espy. And you should talk – you, spending quality time with Offs, maybe?"

I said not a word; she looked up – she was crying. Then she bolted from her chair and she was out the door.

I caught up to her at the Pit. The place stayed open, just as a reminder, I think, and to freak out the recruits. But it was empty and dark, with only running lights on. The smell of stale blood and sweat permeated the place. What with the shadows and the weapons just waiting for a hand, for some, this space was a little forget-me-not of woe; for others, it was the appetizer for the main course of actual combat. At that point, for just a bit longer, I was somewhere between those two camps in this void.

Not a complete void; there was Tango. She was on the floor, sitting at the guardrails with her legs dangling through the rails over the edge.

I sat down beside her. Her voice was low, with all the calm after the storm, thick – with all the last bits of rain that had fallen – and would fall again.

"Little girls ... little whores ... mothers ... sisters ... widows – what we do – *in the company of men*. We smile when we don't mean it; we cry when we ... cry. We wish. We hate. We watch – we wait. We fight – we kill. We forgive. See what we learn to do – in the company of men."

I looked around, at the dark walls, at the blood down there, black on the weapons we used so readily, so often they were just another set of utensils.

"Tango ..."

She stopped me.

"Vache is gone. He's gone, Espy. They say he got shipped out – at least, that's what they say."

Quality time, my ass; I knew what I needed now.

I found a way to get my name added onto the training roster in the Pit schedule when neither Decatur or Diamond were spotting. It wasn't hard; the attending Officer knew I was fit for a lot more than some close hand work.

So I went into the Pit with another squad – and there was Djan. Hard to say if it was relief on his face as he saw me, but he made a beeline for me. Again, it was smoke and mirrors; again, we did the dance of near death for the Officers up at the rail. We did a good job until I could get out the words that no one else would hear, down on the floor grappling with him over the ownership of a truncheon.

"Djan – we're missing a recruit."

"You are."

"He shipped out?"

He slammed me across the head with his hand; I kneed him, rolling him onto his back. We fought some more, closer, harder.

"No," he said.

"Where is he?"

"Gone."

"You saw?"

"A friend did. In the sick-bay."

My punch set him back on his heels.

"Can't be. Your kind gets sewn up in its own wing."

There was real pain in his eyes; he slapped me hard – I had it coming.

"Your boy wasn't in your sick-bay. He was in mine."

This stunned me; I dropped my guard and Djan threw me across the floor. The Offs were treated apart, for good reasons. No mixing; our sick-bay was off limits to any but Base personnel. Djan caught up with me; his kick went into my hand and I toppled him beside me. Once more, those golden eyes were right there in my face.

"They dragged your boy into our sick-bay. He was fighting for his life – right up to the second the neuro shot took him down."

We were both up on our feet, now – I was sick with horror. I was blind with it, blind with that anger again, that rage. Both my hands went into one fist across his face and I brought him to the floor; Djan went down again, dragging me with him.

"He never came out, Espy. He didn't leave there alive."

My fist went back – and the Officer shouted.

"Time!"

We got up; golden eyes stayed on me as I turned and left the arena.

It was later, in my room and Tango had heard all I cared to tell her about what I knew. That Vache had been killed – retired – by our side, by our people.

The reason was in front of us both — the files that Vache had somehow found and pirated — files we had looked over for the umpteenth time.

"They're gone, Tango. All of last year's — and before."

What the files held was lading slips — inventory dates, sales numbers — except in this case, the inventory was recruits. How this place managed to get away with it, I'll never know. Who exactly was running the operation; same. But every team, every recruit, for every season in the last decade — had been sold — as fighters, as hit teams, as gladiators — as worse. We weren't going to see any of them, none from the prior year or any year — unless we ended up in the unit they served in now, in whatever kill squad they were being deployed, scattered from one end of the Rim to the other.

They either served — or they died.

They were gone — so would we be soon.

The name on the sign off sheets was Diamond's.

We sat, both too sick, too full of it to speak. And in me it rose again – the anger. But this time it wasn't there by itself; I was there, in there with it – in control.

The shoes were falling everywhere now.

I saw Tango only twice after that. We trained once with the Chief; I met her over a drink. Then – she was gone. It didn't take more than one or two more sessions in the Pit; she didn't show. Not in her quarters – a new recruit answered the door. He didn't know squat about who'd bunked there before him. He was scared enough to invite me in for talk and whatever else that bunk might offer. I passed on his offer, I calmed him down; I lied – I was getting real good at this kind of front by now. But I was still in a cold sweat when I got back to my own quarters. This place had never felt safe; now, it was infinitely less so.

Suddenly it seemed darker and lonelier than ever before, much more dangerous since that day long ago when I stood my ground, the day I saw a trophy in the Chief's office – an office with no files anywhere in sight. And my eyes went to that sofa …

My next visit was to Engineering Ops. I made a point of getting into the Lab; suddenly I wanted to know everything there was to know about the doors that led to the tunnel, to the Off's cells – how they closed, how they were opened. I smiled and chatted; in less time than you can say scared shitless, I walked out of the Lab with a remote that would do what I needed – and I kept that thing on me. Not sure what I was thinking; I should have known something was coming up that next day.

There was no formal training on schedule; yet there it was in my inbox – the Chief wanted me in the Pit at 23:00. We never trained that late; there was no cc to Quartermaster or any other Officers.

With a cold knot in my stomach, I found Cos, Poli and whoever I still felt close to. They knew what I knew about Vache – soon more and more recruits would know, too. I passed the word; I didn't know what would happen. All I knew was that we had to win – even if it made us even more valuable – as product.

I geared up.

I got to the Pit; I got there early – there was stuff I needed to do. There was no sign of Decatur.

I had time to turn around twice – and out of the shadows stepped Diamond.

He was setting up for a training round; he wasn't wearing armor. He'd laid out short bludgeons and knives on the floor. I didn't like the look in his eye when I walked up to him because there wasn't one. Whatever he had in mind, there was no sign – except in his body language. Tense, this guy was tense; the way you get tense when you've something scratching in your mind other than what you got your hands on right now. When he smiled, the hair lifted on the back of my neck.

I half-smiled back. I put a lot of care into that smile; like cold steel, it stayed frozen on my lips, like a death mask – like the half-smile some lunatic had chiseled into the dead face of the Off in Decatur's office.

"A few night moves, Diamond? Where's the Chief?"

His eyes left me; he tossed a bludgeon stick to me.

"Not coming; he sent me."

He was lying; I knew it and he knew I did.

"We're bumping up your training a notch," he said.

He started out slow; that freaked me, he was clearly testing. It was one thing to see me from the guardrail above the arena, quite another to be across from me there on the floor. He tossed one thrust after another, increasingly forceful and ever closer to my face and torso.

"Keep that guard up! Watch your left."

It was all part of a plan; his remarks were there for one thing only – as distraction. I ignored them, I needed to focus – another shoe was coming.

He parried my next thrust; I took a big chance. I let him get hold of my shirt. He threw me across the floor; there was a lot of information in that move. I came to a stop and gambled again – he was watching me like a hawk – I let him catch a breath as he slowly came closer.

"I figured Tango would be here with us," I said. What had passed for a smile on his face vanished. Slowly, carefully, I was up, walking a big circle, always around him, always keeping him out of range.

"Why's that?" he said finally, and the hair lifted at the sound in that voice. He knew where I was going; he let me go there anyway. It wasn't a question he'd asked, it was the next step.

"She's so much better at this than I am – we could take this to a whole other level." Then I waited, I wanted to see where his eyes went – they stayed down on the weapon in his hand – he'd switched out to a blade. He tossed that knife at my face; I caught it but the game had changed. Those cold eyes stayed on me, on the new blade he picked up, as he told me what I already knew.

"I thought you knew; she shipped out, just a day ago. She wanted me to say she'd be in touch as soon as she got her legs under her."

He looked full into my face; we both knew where we both stood. I continued my circle; then I lunged in quick and my blade raked across his shoulder. A wet red line soaked through his shirt.

"You made two mistakes," he said. "You came alone – and you didn't make a crippling stroke."

He lunged at me; I parried, I wanted this to last as long as I could make it, and this time I caught him across his knife hand. His voice was thick with rage; there was death in that voice now, clear as day.

"You arrogant little bitch. You think it's going to make a difference?"

"As in us being product, what you sell on the market, Diamond? Tango got in the way, didn't she – did she see it coming?"

"Neither will you."

It was all out now; I never dropped guard for a second. He was going to kill me there if he could. My job now was to tire him – I was faster, I was younger. I was scared – but he was desperate, and his assumption that my fear would cripple me was wrong. Because the anger had come back – there it was and I let it roll over me like a wave – except this time, for the first time, I wasn't going to let it wash me away. It was like a song in me; what I said to Diamond was what I'd said to Tango on one of the first days we'd met and it was Tango's voice I heard in my head.

"You tell us that this is all we've got. It isn't. You tell us that if we sell out here, somehow it's a good thing, that we'll make it elsewhere. The enemy isn't in the Pit. You're the enemy – the enemy within, the leaders who lead us to self destruction, the teachers of lies – the only lives you're saving are your own."

I got cut up bad; I cut him up worse. In five he was breathing hard, with one mistake after another. I backed him to the wall, I wanted him to see how it would go – we neither of us saw what was happening at the entry gate to the Off's tunnel, to the cells.

One by one, the Offs had come to the bars; one by one, they'd lined up there, watching, because they knew what was happening here in the Pit – and there at the very front, his hands gripped tight on the bars – was Djan.

Diamond was in a rage.

"She's in sickbay now; waiting to die. You won't get that far – you're going down here."

"Could you speak a little louder, Diamond – *because you're on system wide intercom – right now*," I said. That, of course, was why I had needed to come early; I had turned on the intercom.

The explosion took us both by surprise; one second I was going in for my kill, the next the floor rocked under our feet and the walls shook – and alarms began to sound everywhere. Somewhere other than here was terribly wrong – it was an attack on the Base itself. Diamond seemed oblivious to it; all he wanted was to see me dead, right there. He stepped back, skidded on his own blood and his legs shot out from under him. He had just enough left to throw his knife straight at me; I pivoted, slammed it away, and I went down, too.

The next thing I knew he was over me; he made one mistake. He went for my knife, not my throat. We wrestled until I tossed the thing away and I went for him bare handed. But he was taller, heavier; in a heartbeat, he had me in the killing spot – with all my effort, I pulled out the remote I carried and slammed it down as Diamond's hands found my throat.

He never saw it coming – Djan had run forward, through the open gate, and had Diamond by the neck. The other Offs had gotten out, too; but it was Djan who cut Diamond's throat with his own knife. Djan threw him off me – his hand came down to me – and he pulled me up. I was stumbling, but we all went to the lockers, pulling out more gear, more weapons.

I don't know what was in my head; I owed this place nothing, I just didn't want to die here at the hands of the kill squads, the mercenaries that had attacked us, that had as their only agendas getting our intel and hardware. Neither did the Offs. We climbed out of the Pit, ran to the door and into the corridor – to find Poli and Cos and Crush there, all armed, with the rest of the squads.

For only a second, their eyes went wide at the sight of the Offs – then my squad laughed – they got it.

"Tell me what we got, Cos; break it down," I shouted over the din in the hallway.

"They hit us on decks Eight and Four, not much more – Engineering and shuttle bays spared. We have minimal to no shields; about 20 armed enemy targets were spotted – all mercenaries. They're headed toward Comm – floor by floor."

"Can we intercom selectively?" Djan asked.

"Yeah," I said. "I see where you're going, Djan."

We sent a little message to whomever was listening on select channels – we would come into them from the neighboring levels. But what would we do when we got there?

Djan went back into the Pit; he shot back through the door to us – and Diamond's severed head was hanging, dripping blood, from his hand.

"As of right now, you recruits are our prisoners," he said.

That's how he saw it; that's how it played. You don't need to hear the particulars.

We made our way to the point where all recruits put their hands on their heads, where we made visual with the enemy. That enemy was ready to bring us down – until they saw the head, the head of what might have been the Base CO in the hand of an Off. With a look of real delight, their commander came forward – he was looking ahead, to the bounty he might claim on us, to the trophy in Djan's hand – he was smiling right up to the moment the game changed and we stormed into them – and killed the commander where he stood.

It was the same on the other decks; our teams stayed covert and helpless until it was too late for anyone to suspect otherwise. Then we were in full sight and helpless no longer. Those who had thought to take us easy found we were not easy, not ready to be taken as planned.

We went deck by deck for survivors. We cleaned up; sent a coded message out to Command. I knew for sure that whatever Officers we didn't find in pieces in the corridors had vacated the Base – that included Decatur. We had shuttles; we had pilots. The Offs – they were as unsure as we were where we were headed next. But we had defended our own; we had as good a story to tell as any higher-ups might want to hear.

We would decide that later.

For now, I had somewhere to go.

Djan got me into the Off's sickbay – it didn't take us long to find Tango. She was still on a table; she was hurt bad.

I went to her; I took up her hand, I kissed her forehead. She had just enough left to smile at me.

"Did I miss the fun, Espy?"

"No; you *are* the fun, Tango."

Her face was white; it was hard for her to talk now.

"Espy, I want to send a message – to my sister, I want to tell her …"

She couldn't finish the sentence; so through my own tears – I did.

"I'm going to tell her how good a *real* soldier you are. I'm going to tell her that you're the winner, now. I'm going to tell her how much you loved her."

I would deliver that message personally.

The smile stayed on her face as life left her eyes.

I closed those eyes; I took off her tags, put them into my shirt next to my heart – and Djan and I left for our shuttle.

THE KNIFE

"The Villa has been here since 1600. But we have traced parts of it to a much older time. At its heart, it is as old as the Town itself. And the heart, of course, this is the most important thing. What do you think, Signorina Bardi?"

The old man stood silent for a moment. Narrowed against the bright sunlight, his grey eyes, washed pale with time, studied the girl before him. She wore no hat today. The smooth curve of her throat was as creamy white as the richly worked lace of her silk blouse, with only a translucent tracery of pearl blue veins glowing through the porcelain skin, just at the edge of the collar. Standing there in the warm Umbrian sun, she had loosened her jacket, pushing back lapels whose velvet edges were the colour of fallen leaves at season's end, exactly the shade of the well-cut skirt and hand-sewn shoes. Under her arm, she held close the small journal finely bound in burnished, well-worn Moroccan leather. Her gloves hung loose in hands that glowed like alabaster.

At this time of year, even the mornings were warm. The air was already fragrant with an aerial tisane of pungent herbs and burgeoning blooms. By afternoon, the racing sun would catch the Palazzo in the ancient Town below them. The stones would grow rosy, blushing under the midday heat that pulsed down like a golden stream, insistent as any lover. Then at twilight, while the sky above sank into sapphire reverie, the stones would cool, darkening to drowsy lavender and magenta, as if in shame at the memory of the sun's hungry lustre.

Restless under his watchful gaze, the girl stepped forward to stare upward. The wide face of the house with its many high, corniced windows, had its firm back nestled solidly, comfortingly, against the hills which hung over the town of Gubbio itself. If the hamlet seemed to slumber below, the Villa seemed ready to awaken, like one caught unexpectedly between rousing and sleeping. Like one struggling against the bonds of fever's dreams.

Her voice, soft and musical, rose over the languid hum of bees and soothing cadence of birdsong floating upward to them from the terraced gardens that spread, rank on emerald rank, down the hill toward Gubbio.

"Yes, Signor Foro. The heart is the most important thing," she said.

"Bardi. Bardi; it is Italian. An old and respectful name; but for an Englishwoman? There was a family here, once. Long ago."

"Yes. My grandfather. He was born here... near Gubbio." She became silent under his eyes, eyes infinitely more penetrating as he took her in, as he now tried to place the child of a vague past in the present young woman.

"Ah. Then that explains it. The eyes, yes...the eyes, Signorina."

And she lowered hers, suddenly shy before his certainty. The old man was touched; by her shyness, by the sudden, undeniable vulnerability in the young woman's eyes and stance.

He gave her his arm. Grateful, as if she were taking hold of a lifeline, she took it. He led her up the stairs of the Villa, toward the welcoming darkness beyond the carven door while, from the road below the house, the sound of a vehicle rose up; the car that had bought her up the winding hill. For a moment, the sound hung, strong and potent, ringing in the air.

Then the hum of its engine changed; like a sigh, it rose, throbbing then waned away, until it was just a soft murmur in the distance.

25 July 1925. Villa Lorenzo, Umbria.
My first entry, having just arrived today into that golden-litten country north of Perugia.

The old house is just as it was so many years ago, full of cupboards, secret passageways. Perhaps its stones are heavier. The men in the village; the same. Their eyes so black, so bright, questing; seeing no doubt one different than the child they saw before. Those eyes like hands over one, ignoring the clothing, seeming to thrust the cloth aside, reaching for the flesh below. No Englishman would look at a woman this way. Dark eyes, dark skin; their arms, naked, muscular, they shine like honey-coloured satin in the warm sun. The call of the bull, a low, muted roar, reaching me from the meadow just below the house. Impatient, he seems; savage, hungry for release. His eyes too, are dark. When Signor Foro asked me how long I would stay, my mind became a blank. I simply had no idea what to say.

Here I am come to forget.

It takes no strength to leave someone, or to be left. It takes strength to forget, when all that memory does contrives to bring the thought of that face, that voice, those eyes, ... back. Like a knife. The narrow, insistent wound it makes each time. Clean. Like tears are clean. But never so sanctifying.

I remember Signor Foro (was his hair always so silver?) has a son and a daughter, both my age. They study in Florence, the son to be an artist. A great sculptor; his voice grows thick with pride as the father speaks of him, of his skill, his hands, his vision. Gentle. Fierce. Is this what vision brings? The daughter – a painful invisibility, a simple shrug of those round old shoulders to my unspoken query. I have seen their rooms, waiting for them, like cenotaphs.

I am alone here in this wing of the Villa. I sit alone in this room, with its bed, with the tapestry, the hanging curtains rich and heavy, the deceitful lace. Enormous; like a crypt, able to imprison any spirit however desperate, however strong.

Am I so desperate? The high casement is open to the night, to the rising moon. Listening, I sit. Alone, I wait.

Here I have come to find again my strength.

My hands on my breasts as I dress for dinner. Like his. Before. I will drink wine; I will drink every spirit that is offered me this night.

Hushed and provident, the distant village bell tolled softly midnight.

Rising from a first, early sleep, she went to shut the wide casement. She stayed, standing for a moment in the cool whisper of the night. The shadowed gardens below breathed out fragrance to the dark. In the fullness of the moon's bright stare, her nightdress, her skin both like snow in that light, the long gold hair loose, lifting gently as she stood there.

Shadowlike, from the stillness behind the heavy curtains at her back, he stepped out –and seized her.

For a moment, she could not breathe for fear, so tight was the one hand over her mouth, the other crushing her against his chest. She felt it, something in that other hand, hard and cold against her ribs. The sharp wet taste of leather in her mouth, pungent as the scent of his gloves; fine, light kidskin, tight over the wide spread fingers.

Then the urgent whisper into her hair, his lips warm against her ear, soft words in a rich stream, low and harsh with threat.

You will not make a sound. You will not resist.

And suddenly, there in the gloved hand before her eyes – the knife, the blade long and sharp, so sharp, so bright in the moon's pale light, wordless and warning: *Be still, be still …*

In a breath, he had pulled her backward, away from the window, across to the bed, to sit hard against him. Still the blade was before her eyes, again the low voice at her ear.

You see this, do you not? We are going to play a game, you and I. If you win, you will live. If you lose … well. But if you are strong, you will win. I am going to ask you a question and remove my hand. You will not cry out. You will be strong. You will answer. Are you strong?

The blade seemed blue before her eyes. The hand was removed. Trembling, her body stayed against his, her voice as low as his.

I am strong.

Not a sound. The game has begun. You will not cry out – your answer?

I will not cry out.

Close your eyes. Do not move. What I hold in my hand will be at your throat.

Her eyes close. The heavy, carved bed shifts as he rises and the white wrists are tied, bound together, a silken pull, so soft, so unyielding *(to the poster? No please, please)*. His fingers, soft as whispers across the skin, at her throat, pulling, pulling the ribbons open. The nightdress falls aside, the gloved hands touch her hips, now at her ankles, pulling, pulling her across until her arms are drawn upward, across the pillows, soft and unprotesting, over her head.

The bed shifts under his weight. A hard pressure of clothed hips rough against the inner, petal soft curves of her bare legs.

Open your eyes.

Darkness shifts to near darkness.

The shadowed figure kneels on the bed between her legs. Masked, some dark fabric, silky, sheer; a glint of eyes *(what colour whose eyes whose?)* from the two rough tears in the obscuring silk. The knife, long ebony-handled blade, gleaming on the counterpane beside her hip; watchful, unfeeling.

The gloved hands reach forward to hover over trembling breasts. Butter-soft leather, feather light across the skin that shakes now, nipples rising against all reason, mocking fear. Hands reach, lowering to caress the smooth hips. The silken touch of his lips, his tongue against a breast; a warm, wet thrill moves across the cool ivory stomach, lowers to the hair curling darkly gold below, now against her inner thigh, warmer than her warmth, soft insistence, tasting, reveling in a terrified salt-sweet.

(No gentle? Why soft what why gentle?)

The low voice is hoarse, shaken now.

Close your eyes.

A single deep breath. Her eyes close to the sound of his breathing, a rustling, the moments counted by heartbeat. Then the weight again, but warm this time, warmth of bare skin, the full weight of him on her, settling, warm, soft, breath on her face; the softest whisper.

Open your eyes.

Hers wide now *(can't move can't)* look into his. Lips like slow, easy satin across her throat, brushing, caressing, at her ear, smooth, naked fingers everywhere, the lightest soft questing, pressing, opening, passing.

Gasping as the lips brushed suddenly across hers. Once, again, lingering now, to brush back, forth, quickening, her own parted, moist, eyes shut against the closeness, the scent of him, the strange warm fear.

And his hands, bare, warm, clinging, suddenly beneath her hips, relentless. To be pulled to him, lifted open, the weight of his thighs over hers as he moves against her, her legs forced completely apart.

26 July 1925.

Kind man, the Constable. Truly shaken with this. As much as Signor Foro; as much as I.

He sits beside me in the solarium, trying to look at me, trying to look away. Leaning forward as I speak; hungry to catch the words, each word. I can remember him kneeling beside the bed, I told him. His lips were very close to my ear.

And then the Constable asked me: Signorina, could I remember anything else? I said I remembered clearly — that he had told me to close my eyes again. But I could not close my eyes; I was afraid, I did not know what he was going to do then; I think I must have cried out.

What did he say to you?

Suddenly I am back there – on the bed, in the night ...

Are you going to hurt me? I asked him. Please...

Are you strong?

Yes.

Then you have won the game. Now close your eyes.

And I did. So still, the room; I felt the breeze over me from the open casement. I opened my eyes. I saw I was alone in the room. And my hands ... my hands were free, the silk, whatever it was that had held them ... it was gone.

So gentle, the Constable's voice, as gentle as his eyes, as pleading, for the words, as the images grow in his mind.

Signorina. I know how difficult this is. I would spare you if I could. What did you do then, Signorina?

I told him that I rose, I covered myself with my robe, I remember crying out as I ran to the door. Violetta, she must have heard me cry out; suddenly, she was there, in the doorway. I fell and she caught me, I must have fainted.

Yes, Signorina, of course you must have fainted. This is also what the maid has said. One last question, Signorina, please forgive me ... this man ... I realise that after such a terrible experience ... this man ... did he ... such an unforgiveable act ... what I mean is, did he ...

The Constable's eyes, burning into me, so bright, so eager.

You are asking ... did he rape me.

Yes, Signorina.

No. There was no ... he never ... No. He did not.

He did not?

No.

The Constable rose and left; he and Signor Foro spoke a great while. The villa grows quiet again.

They can find no trace of him. They ask that I remain at the Villa another day. If I can.

All that next day; waiting. Finally, she would no longer stay abed.

Venturing out, at first tentatively; a spot of white in the shadowed courtyard. Then more steadily, the shoes finding their way across the stones, the wet grass. Pure white shoes treading the new, unfamiliar paths. All in white, she walks, cutting basket on the stainless arm.

The grounds men are different now. Softened, the dark eyes alive with pity, phrases of care, soliciting her with their solicitude. She nods at their voices, so soft; more like boys than men, full grown and strong. Voices rising and falling, voices that awaken memory.

Whose voice whose eyes whose whisper who ...

The workers watch her as she passes, their eyes no longer insistent. Which of them can elevate her highest – the white one, the lady all in white?

27 July 1925.
I dreamt that he returned last night, the one who had loved me.

It was as before, that quiet hour before the bell and as before he was behind me before I was aware. The casement swung free from my hand. Pulled backward against him, this time I turned, I whirled in his arms to face him, unafraid.

Where is your knife? I said.

Knife? I have no knife.

In the silver tray on the dresser, the long, bright letter opener under my hand. I strike at him, his hand suddenly dark; a thin line of blood. The smile on his lips as he takes it from me; my fingers unresisting. He tosses it away.

He reaches for me. Bare hands now on my breasts, kneading, summoning, like hungry flames, burning away the spent, colourless traces of any others before. My mouth stopped with his, the cry swallowed into his own. His mouth a fire against mine, feasting, lips forcing mine apart, his tongue no stranger now, finding its own familiar way, deep, deep into me, thrusting, paring away the memory of any other, like a knife cutting the fruit which waits the blade, paring away, leaving only the ripe, new heart, the sweetest, innermost core. I would not fight against these arms, lifting, enclosing, insistent, calling me downward. I would not fight the hard, hurried parting, his pressing into me, hot, aching, forcing inward, forcing the ready cry from my lips into his, my legs wrapped around him, keeping him there, hard, deep, opening, filling, driving deeper into hot, sweet, completion. And this time he does not stop. I could not, would not have stopped him, had I been able. This time I hunger, famished, I thirst, frenzied, to see what lies on the far side of gentleness. Taken, taking, again, and again, until, swooning, the cold wind plays over me once more. I am still.

Now unfeeling; now feeling everything. At ease. Alive. Alone. Again in sweet, warm darkness.

The poor, poor Signorina Bardi. A lovely young lady.

Such a terrible, terrible thing, thought Violetta.

She had been happy, so happy to help, happy to tell, her voice low, tremulous, how she had heard the cry in the night and run to the Signorina's rooms. How she had come upon her in the doorway, the long hair loosened, tumbling ringlets of gold. The poor Signorina. Her face as white as the rich soft robe over the silken nightdress, such beautiful lace, so delicate. And to think, I was the one who caught her, falling, so cold, so pitiful, senseless with terror. And with shame, no doubt, thought Violetta. Such shame.

Violetta's polished shoes tap primly over the faded tiles. Her thin arms are draped with crisp linen, white and starched as a nun's veil as she pushes open the heavy door to the girl's room. Cool shadows of late day, the scent of fading roses in the smoky glass beside the bench where Violetta sets her linens. Her arms stretch out to open the carved casement, bringing in the cleansing day, airing the close, still room.

The dark eyes come to rest on the bed, come to stare; at the wide, secretive expanse, like clean, new snow. The linens are held tightly in her hands as Violetta halts before the bed.

A border to another land. Forbidden. Sensations, dark, so dark. Warm. Forbidden. Terrible.

The dark gaze bright as it travels across that unfamiliar land.

Her eyes first on the high, ancient posters, sturdy and narrow.

The dark oak arms climb up, reaching even as the Signorina's arms must have reached, held high over her head, that golden head, the river of bright hair tossing side to side. White flesh straining against the bonds. And his hands, hard, strong, knowing, pulling at the white limbs. Holding, forcing. There – the place in the white pure counterpane, where not one but two must have lain. Together. Bare. Pressing. Pushing. And not a sound, not until I found her in the doorway.

The maid's thin hands tremble as Violetta makes the bed.

On the fine oak dresser, the Signorina's letters, unopened, stacked alone in the empty pewter tray. It is gone; I shall bring her another letter opener, thinks Violetta, so the Signorina may open her letters, so she may read them. They will soothe her. Sweet petals of lavender and rose, thin green ribbons of fresh thyme and sage fall sprinkling to the floor, then rustle like whispers, swept hard, briskly into fragrant silence by Violetta's sensible broom. Her thin angular body kneels to a dark spot on the boards. More than one; two, no, three dark drops; drying, sticky. Not like wine; not wine.

Her cloth darkens as she wipes the old boards clean and from the rooms below, the voice of Signor Foro rises to her ears.

"Signorina? Signorina Bardi."

27 July 1925.
"Signorina? Signorina Bardi..."

Awakening in late day's warmth, pushing back the borders of close, dark sleep, struggling against the arms of my chair. Signor Foro is at the library door; he looks down upon me, the white-crowned head tipped, the saintly, sweet regret and pity darkening his eyes to sleet-grey.

"Forgive me, Signorina, I did not see you resting there. But here is someone I am wanting you to meet, you may remember him from long ago.

It is my son. He takes a few days from his studies to ease his old father's loneliness. Piero ..."

Leaning forward now, from behind his father, he steps forward. Tall, wide-shouldered, the dark hair falls forward over the high forehead, the short, graceful bow as he halts above me. The hand extends, taking mine, holding, enclosing; his long fingers as finely chiseled as any work in stone. I stand now to look into the dark, lean face, the smile on the full lips, gentle and faint, as faint and gentle as whispers are in darkened rooms. The low voice, so low, melodic in this shadowed place.

"Signorina Bardi. My father has spoken of nothing else. I have waited for this moment ... when we would meet."

Hearing that voice, saying my name; my hand still captive. Sensation in my palm, tingling, shrinking from the cloth – from the thin, light bandage which is wound about the sculptor's hand.

"You have injured yourself, Sir."

"It is nothing. Passion exacts its own price, in art, as in life. When one wants – desires deeply enough, one risks much. One goes beyond fear, beyond pain – one does not feel it. I would not have refused the moment to spare myself this."

Face to face. Knowing, meeting that look, those eyes. Eyes that are not, in this light, as the father's, not that cool bright grey nor even the keen, flashing darkness of the men in the gardens beyond. Eyes that are something else; something completely unforeseen in this light, in the full light of day.

They walk from the house together. Together, turning to look back at it, solid and comforting. They walk to the rows of heavy vines planted close, the grapes thick and sun- hungry, the vines marching in new green up the stony hill. Walking in silence, the silence that closeness breeds; only to stop.

Reaching into the vest pocket of the fine suit, the long fingers press, searching. To draw out the small penknife, its hilt of carved ivory, meticulously worked, pierced, magical. Opening the blade, he cuts a small bundle of the tiny, clustered fruits, tastes them. Juice shines on the full lips, the smile; the eyes on her again.

"Will it be a good year," she asks.

"Will it? Yes. It will. I know it."

Her eyes on the knife, rapt on the short, bright length of sharp quicksilver in his hand.

"What do you see there? It is a knife. It is only a knife."

Wordless, she gazes up at him, into that bright regard, hearing that soft voice turn suddenly hoarse, suddenly shaken again – with need.

"Stay. I beg you. For one more night."

Her answer in her eyes. Slowly, carefully the blade is folded back to rest once more, silent and unseen in the still, dark bed of his palm – and he hands the richly carved thing to her.

"You are strong. You have won the game."

Her hair like beaten gold in the sun as she watches him turn and walk away, back to the house ...

'Her hair like beaten gold in the sun as she watched him turn and walk away, back to the house.'

"Signorina? Signorina Bardi..."

Her pen hangs, poised above the page. The girl in the back seat of the car looked up at his words. The driver had half-turned toward her and he spoke again.

"We are nearly there. The Villa is just above us, there."

"Thank you."

She closed her journal, running long, white fingers over the worn Moroccan leather, smooth and shining. Setting it down beside her gloves on the seat, she loosened her jacket against the midday heat, the rich cinnamon of the tailored cloth setting off the startling clarity of her porcelain skin. The long gold hair was coiled up; in spite of the warm sun, already high, she would wear no hat today.

Ahead, the road curved sharply; already the house was coming into view, bringing a flood of memories. Today, nothing but the sun on her hair. No hat, not even gloves.

The car pulled to a stop at the bottom of the hill. She left the car, with her bag. Above, Signor Foro, his hair like snow in the bright air, stood waiting before the house as the girl came up to meet him. The driver waited, watching them as they stood together, the old man with her bag in his hand, the girl beside him, like father and daughter, speaking softly.

The driver watched and loosened his collar, as, striding on his long legs through the lower gardens, came the tall young man, crossing to meet the car, his leather bag over his shoulder, a wayward lock of dark hair falling forward over the high forehead.

He looked down on the seat where she had rested only a moment ago and tossed the bag there. He turned, his eyes going back to the house, to the high, corniced windows, to where his father stands, the girl still beside him, now silent and graceful, with her ivory skin, her fair head tilted back, the light on her hair like gold. With the car door open under his hand, he watches as age and youth climb the steps of the Villa, arm in arm.

The driver looked up at him.

"To the village, Signor Piero?"

Still, the young man's eyes follow the old man and the girl for the space of one long breath. His eyes meet those of the driver.

"Perhaps. Then again – perhaps not," said Piero.

"Already the season has changed, Signor Piero. It will be a warm night, I think."

Their eyes meet again and the young man smiles; a smile as faint and gentle as whispers are in darkened rooms.

"Yes," he replied. "A very warm night indeed."